To Sherry Taber;
From our [illegible]
yours - enjoy
Chris Moreau

The Professor's Telescope

A New Edu-Sci-Fi Novel

The Professor's Telescope

by Chris Moreau

Illustrated by Jane Marek

The Professor's Telescope ®

This book is a work of fiction. All of the names, places, characters, and situations are products of the author's imagination. Any relationship to actual events, person's living or dead, or location is entirely coincidental.

This book is printed on Acid-Free Paper.

Library of Congress Cataloging–in–Publication Data

Moreau, Chris, 1958-
The Professor's Telescope / Chris Moreau
ISBN 0-9785399-0-7
1. Science Fiction. 2. Children's Fiction.
I. Moreau, Christina II. Title

MANUFACTURED IN THE UNITED STATES OF AMERICA

The Professor's Telescope
is dedicated to the real Professor.
Your unfailing generosity of time and
knowledge has taught me that the
true joy of astronomy
is sharing the wonders of the
night sky with others.
Thanks Eric!

Contents

Foreword

Silver streamlined rockets clawing their way into the air with thundering engines...incredible energy weapons blasting alien invaders into oblivion...computing machines of immense power and sophistication controlling the workings of whole worlds...political intrigue on a cosmic scale trapping the space-faring hero into saving the universe or dying in the attempt...

These visions of science fiction inspired a generation to become the engineers, technicians and others who sent mankind to the moon. Followers of Star Trek, Star Wars and similar TV shows and movies convinced another generation to explore the solar system with robots, build a space station and design computers, cell phones and other advances in technology that are common today yet were once fantastic devices in someone's wild imagination.

Today's generation is taking on the challenge of returning to the moon and beyond. It's possible that some children living today may be the first earth travelers to land on Mars. Books like "The Professor's Telescope" not only teach science basics but open a child's mind to the infinite possibilities of an idea and will inspire a new generation to reach for the stars.

Jim Draggoo

Executive Director, Kid's Cosmos

Chapter 1

The Professor was strange. That was clear from the beginning. Eric couldn't quite put his finger on the strangeness either. It was the kind of feeling that quivers around inside you; a sort of roller coaster feeling that starts with a queasy stomach and then travels to a headache and a tingly feeling in your fingers and toes. Eric knew the minute he saw the Professor standing at the front of the classroom that there was something unusual about him.

It was Career Day at Roosevelt Middle School. In an effort to get the students excited about signing up for high school classes that spring, the teachers had invited several people from their small community to speak about their professions. Eric had had a hard time choosing between Emergency Medical Technician and Air Traffic Control for the first session, but had finally settled on EMT. It was interesting, but Eric wasn't sure it was for him. He *was* sure that he didn't like the sight of blood!

The second session he attended was so boring he could barely keep his attention on the speaker. It was supposed to be about computer technology, something Eric enjoyed. He really liked using the computers at school and was pretty good at it, too; it had only taken him a few class periods to make a cool PowerPoint presentation for last year's History class. But this lady made computers about as interesting as cleaning his room.

The last session that Eric had signed up for, Veterinary Science, was full. It appeared that half the girls in the eighth grade wanted to be veterinarians, so his name ended up under something he knew absolutely nothing about; Astronomy. Now here he was.

He was glad but not surprised to see his best friend Meredith Weatherford one row over; her tall, thin frame folded uncomfortably into one of those chair/desk combinations his school was fond of buying. They were brightly colored and modern looking but not fit to sit in, especially if you had giraffe legs like hers. Meredith was here by choice Eric supposed, because to her Astronomy was at least more interesting than cleaning her room. Or being a veterinarian.

She waved a familiar hello. He waved back weakly while the butterflies-in-the-stomach feeling continued to build inside him.

Meredith was wearing her favorite T-shirt especially for the occasion. At first glance, the design on her shirt appeared to be a random scattering of stars on a field of black, but at closer inspection the stars revealed their true purpose; to outline the facial features of none other than Albert Einstein. For further novelty, the shirt glowed in the dark, so the effect that it created was that of a weirdly glowing mad scientist lunging at you from out of the night. It was an effect that Meredith obviously relished because she wore the shirt every chance she got.

In contrast, the Professor wore a lab coat like the one Mr. Kincaid, his Biology teacher, wore. But Mr. Kincaid's coat was usually spotted and splashed with things that Eric could only guess at. His classmates often speculated about what the mysterious substances were. Some said it was the evidence of that day's You-Guess-What-it-Is cafeteria lunch. His more inventive friends suggested that it might be the remains of last week's frog dissection, or yesterday's interior inspection of a worm's belly. Eric had the suspicion that they only said that to gross out the girls who were within earshot. It always worked.

The lab coat that currently was at the front of the classroom with the unusual Professor inside was as white as a cloud. It was so clean and spotless that the April sun streaming through the window made it difficult to look at. The man's hair, a trifle shaggy, hung down past the collar of his coat. He had a long, sad face, like someone who had seen more than his fair share of trouble. But it was his eyes that caught Eric's attention and held it; tired eyes whose direct stare swept the classroom before settling uncomfortably on Eric. The boy could not help staring back.

Then the man smiled. Although it did nothing to hide the sadness, it was a smile filled with the same light that was coming through the window. When he spoke his voice was surprisingly quiet for such a large man, and yet his words were filled with so much energy that even when he turned away from the class to put up several photographs Eric could still hear him clearly.

Once the Professor's back was turned the power of his mysterious gaze was broken and Eric could concentrate on the photographs. Colorful wheels of light spun before his eyes. Clusters of bright pinpoints and great spheres of orange and blue that he supposed represented stars and planets hung suspended from the classroom chalkboard, but Eric could not equate anything he saw there with the small black and white pictures that he'd seen in his sixth grade science book. Forget Veterinary Science, this was cool! No wonder Meredith was hooked on this stuff!

The Biology room became a universe where worlds collided. Earth and moon soon made way for galaxies and gaseous nebulae. Crashing meteors created huge, planet changing holes and entire populations of animals became extinct. Ancient civilizations cringed in fear as Venus, Jupiter, and Saturn aligned in the night skies of long ago. Almost before they knew it, the whole class was sucked into a black hole of scientific discussion. Hypotheses and theories about space travel and aliens were hurtling around the classroom like flying saucers in an old science fiction movie. Time hurtled by as well and too soon, the last bell of the day was ringing, bringing the students first back to earth and then into the science room again.

Eric stayed at his desk, stunned by what he had heard. This is amazing, he thought to himself. Why didn't our teachers ever tell us any of this stuff before? How come I've never seen pictures like this? Suddenly, the thoughts that were zooming at light speed inside Eric's head came to a screeching halt. In the picture of Saturn that the Professor had used during his lecture, the planet's beautiful rings were turning serenely before his unbelieving eyes. He blinked a few times, trying to make the image look again like the still photograph it was, but Saturn's rings just kept spinning like a child's toy.

Conversation around him made Eric aware that the lecture had come to an end. At the same time he realized he was being watched intently from a corner of the classroom. He tore his eyes away from the planetary image and turned slowly in his seat until he located the source of the uncomfortable observation. The Professor was staring at him again!

There was a slight frown on his face. Not the type of frown one wears when angry, only a frown of deep concentration or maybe worry. Why would the Professor be worried about me, he wondered. Why would he be thinking about me at all?

"Eric! What on earth is the matter with you?"

Eric whipped his head around.

Meredith stood glaring down at him. She readjusted her thick glasses higher on her nose. "I've been trying to get your attention . . ." The sunlight gave red highlights to her brown braids which were so long they nearly brushed the surface of his desk.

"You scared me!" He looked up at his friend, glad that she now blocked his view of both the strange guest and his equally strange pictures. He'd had enough of ghostly spinning planets for one day. "What did you think?"

Meredith plopped into the chair next to him. "It was a great lecture. Even better than the one I went to at the university last year. I thought –"

"Not about the lecture, silly! About him – the Professor!" Eric whispered the last two words, nodding in the direction of the subject in question.

Meredith grinned. She knew exactly what Eric had been referring to, but enjoyed the chance to tease him once in a while.

"Odd, isn't he?" She scooted closer to guard their conversation, although no one remained in their corner of the room.

"Odd isn't exactly the word I'd use. Scary is more like it. And did you see the-," he swallowed hard, not sure if he wanted to continue. He liked Meredith. They had been friends since the fifth grade and he had no intention of spoiling that now. But if he told her he'd seen the photo of Saturn doing a perfect imitation of a top, he was afraid Meredith would think he was crazy. She'd had other reasons to consider him a nutcase during their long association, but this would surely be the final proof. He needn't have worried.

"—the pictures!" She finished his sentence. "You saw them, too? Thank goodness! I just saw the optometrist a few weeks ago so I knew my eyes couldn't be the problem! Was it only that picture of M51 or were the others moving, too?"

"M-who?" Too excited to wait for an explanation, Eric continued. "How do you think he did that? Was it magic? "

"There's no such thing as magic," declared Meredith loftily. "It had to be a trick of some kind. He's probably some charlatan that Mr. Kincaid dragged in. Is there a carnival in the area, I wonder?"

"I wish you wouldn't do that."

"Do what?" asked Meredith, puzzled.

"Use big words that nobody can understand."

"What? You mean 'charlatan'? A charlatan is a fake-"

"I know what it is!"

"But you just said-"

"I know what I said. But you're sneaky. You slip words in. Big lumpy words into every conversation."

Meredith gave him a look that would fry eggs. "I can't help it. Words are the tangible representation of what's going on inside a person's head."

"Maybe I don't always want to know what's going on inside your head. And there you go again, using big lumpy words that make me feel stupid."

"I'm sorry. I don't do it on purpose," said Meredith.

"I know, but it bugs me. Do it to other people so they can feel stupid."

Eric stopped short. The Professor had finished packing away his pictures, had spoken a few words to the teacher, and was now making a bee line down the aisle toward them! Had he heard them, Eric wondered? Oh, no! He was stopping!

"Did you enjoy the photographs?" It was an innocent enough question, asked in the Professor's gentle voice, but the meaning was clear. He *knew* they had seen the moving pictures. He had *wanted* them to see. He was *glad* they had seen. Eric was sure the man was waiting for them to come right out and admit that they had seen the incredible. But he could not make his brain form any kind of an answer and, wouldn't you know it? Just like a girl, Meredith had chosen this important moment to clam up!

The Professor didn't seem to notice that the two of them were sitting there wordlessly. He just smiled that same filled-with-sunshine-and-sadness smile that he had smiled before. He placed a small business card on the desk in front of them and tapped it once with one of his long fingers. Then he seemed to forget that he'd put it there. He seemed to forget that the children were there, too, as he gazed out through the classroom window at the bright afternoon.

"Astronomy is a fascinating subject, isn't it?" Then, before they could think of a reply, intelligent or not, he was gone.

Meredith was the first to break the spell of silence. "What was that all about?" she asked in an awestruck voice.

Eric gingerly picked up the card between two fingers and read it first to himself, then out loud, trying to make sense of the words.

Dr. Arthur J. Strang Ph.D.
Professor of Astronomy
"You're always safe with the Professor."

Chapter 2

Eric and Meredith stood on the walkway in front of the school, the late afternoon sunshine warming their shoulders. A light breeze ruffled Eric's sandy colored hair and then traveled on to raise the corners of their tattered notebooks. They made an interesting pair as they bent over the Professor's card and studied it carefully, as if it were more likely to give up its secrets in the light of day.

"Always safe," read Meredith. "I wonder what that means."

"Beats me," Eric shrugged.

A few straggling students, who had been in the Astronomy session with them moments before, passed them by, laughing and talking. Meredith watched them until they went around the corner and out of sight.

"Can you believe it?" She was whispering even now. "Those guys didn't see a thing. They're going home like nothing happened. I always thought they were dumb, but gee whiz!"

"I don't think they're dumb, just –, "Eric paused to gather his thoughts.

"Just what?" she prompted.

"Well, just left out, I guess. I mean, the Professor *wanted* us to see those pictures, right?" he explained. "What if he wanted *just us* to see them? Us and nobody else?"

"Why would he show them to 'just us'?"

"I don't know! Do you think I'm a mind reader?" Eric snapped. He didn't mean to take out his frustration on her. He was confused and little scared. He didn't like feeling that way and he didn't want Meredith to know he felt that way, either. That was enough to make him angry, another feeling he didn't want to deal with right now.

"I'm sorry, Meredith, but this is way too weird. I don't understand any of it. Maybe we've been watching too many Sci-Fi movies. Hey! Maybe he chose you because you're an astronomy nut or something."

Meredith shot a dangerous look in his direction. Sometimes she suspected that even Eric thought she was a nerd, just because she wanted to know everything there was to know about space. All right, maybe astronomy *was* an unusual hobby for a girl. Maybe she did go a little overboard telling everybody everything she knew about it. That was no reason for the names kids called her: Bookworm! Four eyes! Nerd! She hated it! Usually Meredith enjoyed a chance to stick up for herself and her hobby, and rarely lost an opportunity to do it. But she resented the necessity of defending herself to her best friend.

"I'm not 'an astronomy nut or something'," she mimicked him crabbily. "I just like learning about it, and that's not the same thing! Besides, he chose you, too. And you don't even like Astronomy. Well, that just shows what poor taste he has!" She smiled a little to take the sting out of her words.

While Eric considered this, he turned the card over in his hand. On the back, printed in letters so small he could barely read them, was an address.

Dr. Arthur J. Strang
W. 3014 Mountain Lane
Durango, Colorado

The address wasn't very far from Eric's own house.

"Did you notice that the Professor's name is strange?" asked Meredith.

"What's so strange about it?" Eric flipped the card to the front side again.

"Not strange meaning weird. Strange meaning the way it's spelled. S-T-R-A-N-G," she explained.

"I don't think it's pronounced that way, though." Eric was better at Language Arts than he was at Math or Science, although he hid the fact fairly well from most of his friends. "Strang without the 'e' – wouldn't that be like Tang – you know, the breakfast drink?"

"Oh, yeah. Tang. Like the astronauts drank on the Apollo missions to the moon."

" Did you notice that the professor's name is strange? "

Eric narrowly avoided rolling his eyes. "Sure, whatever."

"So what are we going to do, now?" asked Meredith.

"Do? Well, I have to go home and get started on my homework. I've got a paper that's due in History on Friday and – "

"I don't mean that! What are we going to do about the Professor?" Gosh, she thought, sometimes boys could be so dense!

"Do?" Eric repeated with a blank look on his face. "About the Professor?"

"Yes! Do! Wake up, Eric! I mean, he comes here to our school with these fantastic photographs that move on their own, and even though they're probably some gag product he picked up at the local magic store, for some reason which I can't explain, we're the only ones that can see them. And then he gives us this card for who knows what reason, and -"

"Geez! Take a breath, will ya? What are we *supposed* to do?"

"Well, shouldn't we report him or something?" Meredith's eyes were wide and bright with excitement behind her thick lenses.

Eric made an explosive noise that sounded like a laugh with all the humor taken out.

"Report him? Report him to who? And for what? As far as we know, he hasn't done anything wrong. And who in their right mind would believe us?"

Eric thought again of the events of the past hour; the amazing spinning planets and galaxies, the lively discussion that had gone on between the Professor and the students; students who often sat bored out of their skulls in the back of the class. Most of all he thought about the Professor himself. The man's intense interest had made him feel anxious and confused, yet at the same time he felt the stirrings of a wondrous anticipation inside him. His whole person tingled in expectation of what the Professor might do next. Something important was about to happen; more important than anything that had ever happened to him in his short, uninteresting, life.

He sighed and shoved the card resolutely into a notebook in his backpack.

"You're right, Eric," said Meredith. "I'm not even sure *I* believe us. We'll have to solve this mystery by ourselves."

They were both silent as they walked home, each buried in thoughts of their own.

* * * * * * *

Eric lived on the south side of town at the end of a road that was thickly lined with trees. It was a nice house, pretty much like the houses his friends lived in with three bedrooms, two bathrooms, a roomy kitchen, and a large family room, only there wasn't a large family to fill it.

Eric often wished he had a brother or a sister. He would even have put up with a pesky little sister like the one Meredith had. It was lonely with just himself and his mom. He really couldn't recall a time when his dad had been in the house. Oh, he remembered his dad, all right. He could picture his face, hear the sound of his voice. When Eric was ten, they had moved from Idaho because the bank his mom worked for had transferred her here and his dad had been hired as a high school math teacher. They had only lived in this house a few months before his dad had been killed in a car accident.

Mom had a hard time when Dad died. They'd left all their friends behind in Idaho and the bank had only given her two weeks off. Then he had started as a new student in fifth grade, met Meredith, and they had quickly become friends.

Even now, Eric didn't like to think about his dad. The only thoughts he had were 'what if's' – what if we'd never moved here? Maybe the accident would never have happened. What if he'd been able to be in Dad's math class next year? What if Dad were here right now? What advise would he give about the Astronomy session and the unusual Professor?

Eric sighed. What good did it do to even think about it? None of it was going to happen, now. And he sure didn't want to tell Mom. She had enough to worry about as it was. No, the events of this afternoon will have to stay just between me and Meredith, he thought. Eric's mom always listened to him and was a good sport about most things, but there was no way she would buy this story. Meredith's mom and dad were okay, too, but he knew that their minds were not exactly the stretchable kind either.

As he passed by the mailbox Eric stopped to get the mail. There were the usual advertisements, bills and things. His grades from the last quarter were in an important looking envelope from the school. Eric was glad that he didn't have to hide them from his mom – he was a better than average student who earned mostly A's and B's. He knew some kids at school who would go to great lengths to hide their grades from their parents. He had even heard of a kid last year who had hacked into the school's computer system and changed his mailing address! It might have worked, if the dummy hadn't accidentally used the address of a guy that worked for his dad. Wow! Was he in trouble once the school got everything sorted out!

As he stuffed the letters into his backpack, Eric realized that he had missed something that was pushed way back to the deepest, darkest part of the mailbox. Reaching in, his hand touched a smooth, rectangular surface. A cold shiver traveled from the top of his scalp to the tip of his toes, causing every hair in between to stand straight on end. He *knew* that feeling! It was the same crawly feeling he'd had in the Astronomy session. The Professor's card! The Professor had been right here at his mailbox! In front of his house! Suddenly Eric's brain, which had been doing a perfectly spinning imitation of Saturn, skidded to a halt.

He pulled out the card and stared at it. It was identical to the one the Professor had handed him that afternoon. It was impossible that a card like this could be here, in his mailbox. It was so impossible, that Eric wildly threw his backpack on the ground and ripped his notebook from it, frantically hunting for the other card. It couldn't be that same one, it just couldn't! How could it be?

Eric thought his head had stopped spinning, but it had only taken a slight detour. He shook the notebook, and to his considerable relief, a small card dropped out fluttering to the muddy ground. Picking it up, Eric wiped it clean on his jeans and held the two cards side by side in the fading sunlight. Two cards, thank goodness, exactly alike except for a few mud stains. Eric had come dangerously close to declaring himself completely out of his mind.

I wonder what Meredith will make of this, he thought. He unlocked the side door and hung his coat in the hallway. Setting his backpack at the base of the stairs, he checked the time, trying to calculate how soon he could call Meredith. He figured he had at least five minutes before she would arrive at her house, so he read the note his mom had left for him on the counter in the kitchen. It was her way of letting him know that she wished she could be there when he got home. They had talked a couple of times about getting a dog, but Mom said it wasn't fair to leave a poor dog home alone all day. He was still working on changing her mind. After all, Weatherford's had a dog and he stayed in all day. Maybe they could get a golden retriever like theirs.

He got out the casserole his mom had prepared for dinner and started the oven to heat. He put the mail on the kitchen counter; careful to make sure the Professor's cards went back into his backpack. It wouldn't do for Mom to find them and start asking questions. On the way up to his room another stray thought struck him like lightning, leaving him with his feet straddling three stairs.

How had the Professor known where he lived? I suppose he could have asked the teacher, thought Eric, or looked it up somewhere, but why would he bother? He picked up the phone as he reached his room and dialed Meredith's number. As soon as he heard her voice, he started to feel a little bit better. He knew that she would help him find the answers to his questions, if indeed there were any answers.

"You'll never believe what I found in my mailbox when I got home!" he said.

"Was it small, white, and rectangular?" she asked.

"How did you know?" Eric almost shouted into the phone.

"I was just about to call you. I'd like to pretend I'm psychic, but I found exactly the same thing in my mailbox. Actually, my dad found it. He had a million questions about it, none of which I was prepared to answer. What do you think it means?"

"I don't have a clue, but I'm going to find out." Eric's voice was heavy with determination. "I'm not going to let him scare me."

"How do we know he's even trying to scare us? This might just be his idea of getting our attention." Meredith suggested.

"Well he's got mine, that's for sure. I'm going over there Friday after school, knock on his door, and ask him what he wants."

"Ask him? Just like that?"

"Sure. I mean, you said it yourself. He hasn't committed any crime, at least not that we know of. Are you going with me?"

Meredith was embarrassed to answer. "Um, I'd like to, but I can't. I have a dentist appointment at 4:00 that Mom had to make months ago. There's no way I can miss it. And then we're supposed to go to dinner at my grandmother's afterward. Can't we go tomorrow?

"No. I have that History paper due, remember? Professor or no, I have to get that finished. Everything else will just have to wait."

"What if something else strange happens before then?"

"We'll just have to cross that bridge when we come to it."

Chapter 3

Friday afternoon arrived. No photographs had moved. No business cards had appeared with the name and address of a strange man printed on them. Everything had been as quiet and seemingly ordinary as it had always been at home and at school. Eric had waved at Meredith as she left for her appointment in the Weatherford's VW van.

He sighed. What a time for her to have something else to do. Since their phone conversation the night before last, Eric had wished at least a hundred times that he had not told Meredith his intention to check out the Professor's house. It would be a lot easier to back out now if he hadn't. Right, he thought. I'll just march up to his front door and start demanding some answers.

Still unsure of exactly what he was about to do, but aware that if he didn't leave soon, students arriving for school Monday morning would find him still rooted to this spot, Eric commanded his frozen feet to move. Apparently this act had the effect of thawing his brain as well, because an alternate plan began to form in his mind. He would go home first, drop off his backpack, get a snack, and wait until it was almost dark. Mom had a meeting at the bank and wouldn't be home until late tonight. He could go by the back way to the Professor's house, check things out, and then if everything looked okay he might go up and knock on the door. It wasn't a great plan. It wasn't even a good plan, but Eric liked it a lot better than the 'Front Door' strategy he had suggested to Meredith.

Twilight had just begun to settle into the trees surrounding the house when Eric carefully locked the door behind him. He carried a flashlight in his back pocket and one of the business cards that had the name and address of the Professor in his hand. Around his neck were his dad's binoculars, a talisman against his uncertainty. He walked down his lane all the way to the end. If he had continued straight ahead, he could have approached the Professor's house by way of a series of well lighted streets. But while that route would have been consistent with the 'Front Door' plan, it was much too visible for what Eric now had in mind.

To his right was a large fenced-in field, where horses were pastured in the summer time. Here the road turned into a narrow lane that was really no more than a path with grass growing down the middle. If he followed this, it would lead him all the way across the meadow to a trail that wound out to the bluff. Judging from the address on the card, the Professor's house should lie on the edge of this bluff, at the far end of Mountain Lane. Eric's new plan required that he cross the field and enter the back of the Professor's property. He would sneak through the trees and get a look at the house. From there he could find out a lot of things.

The number one thing he was interested in learning was whether Professor Strang was actually at home. He couldn't confront the man if he wasn't there, and Eric had no trouble admitting to himself what a welcome reprieve that would be. He could just sneak back home and no one would be the wiser.

As soon as Eric had reached the back yard, he realized that what had seemed like a good scheme was in reality about the dumbest idea he'd ever had! He couldn't see a thing from back here. He couldn't even be sure if it was the right house!

The area where Eric stood couldn't be considered a backyard by normal standards. It was a forest, really, filled with small leafless trees growing very close together. The back of the house was visible, but the few windows that faced the small woods were all dark. He scanned them with the binoculars, but they didn't help him see anyone or anything moving inside. At the right end, the house was taller, like a tower, almost. The top was a rounded, white dome with what looked like a seam that ran all the way from back to front. Even the Professor's house was weird!

Through the trees, pieces of sky were visible, clear and cold. Tiny pinpoints of light winked at him through the trees. Eric shivered, although he was not sure if it was from the cold or the fact that he was playing back yard super sleuth. He wished he'd thought to wear a warmer coat. Circling the trees, he tried to get as close to the base of the tower as he could without being seen from the windows of the house. If he could just make his way around to the front, maybe he could get a look at the house address.

"Fine evening for a little observing, don't you think?" A voice came out of the shadowy silence somewhere to his left.

Eric whipped around. There, leaning against a tree no more than two feet away stood a man. He was cloaked in darkness, but Eric would have recognized that voice anywhere. Certain that he had found the right house, Eric was also certain he was in big trouble. His plan had not included getting caught!

Close up, the Professor was even taller than he remembered. Tonight he had traded the white lab coat for jeans and a heavy sweater, but the change made him no less imposing to the frightened boy. Eric tried to speak, but his tongue was thick and uncooperative, and it was all he could do to keep from swallowing it. He glanced around nervously, but there was nowhere to run.

"Observing?" he finally managed to squeak.

The Professor was quiet for a moment. "Bird watching, perhaps?" He stepped nearer and tapped the binoculars, laughing quietly. "You know, some people use those things for a better purpose." Now he pointed up toward the darkness above them, but Eric could not take his eyes from the man's face.

"You have questions," continued the man. "Many of them, I'd guess."

Eric nodded.

"Well, have no fear, my young friend; your curiosity will be satisfied in time. But it would be a shame to waste such a beautiful evening."

Bewildered, Eric allowed himself to be guided around the side of the house and away from the sheltering trees, still positive there would be some serious repercussions as a result of his backyard spy mission.

The house faced a wide forested valley. Situated there on the high bluff, nothing blocked the huge expanse of sky that spread itself out before them. The hundreds of pinpoints of light that Eric had seen through the trees had now become thousands. Millions. Eric's breath caught in his throat again, no longer out of fear, but in wonder.

"Look, Eric. Orion, Cassiopeia, the Pleiades, Corvis." As he pointed out each arrangement of stars, the Professor sounded as if he were introducing a room full of old and dear friends. Eric listened in spellbound uncertainty as the strange names lingered in the still air.

Sensing the boy's confusion, the Professor responded, "Let me explain. These star formations, called constellations, are named for people and animals in ancient folklore and mythology. Think of the sky as a map of these shapes and you can locate far away objects such as gaseous nebulae and galaxies or objects nearer to Earth like Jupiter or," the Professor pointed to a large unblinking orb high above them, "Saturn."

Relieved to finally hear a name he recognized, Eric pounced on the word.

"Saturn!"

"Here, let me show you." He indicated a convenient bench and they both sat down. Then he took the binoculars and, without removing them from around Eric's neck, held them up. "Now, look at the planet with your eyes, and then swing the binoculars up without lowering your gaze." He demonstrated as he was speaking.

"I don't really see – oh! Is that it?"

"Yes, that's it."

"How come it's not twinkling?"

"A planet can only reflect the light of its sun. A star makes its own light, and when that light enters the earth's atmosphere, it is split into elements of the spectrum. The

" Look Eric. Orion, Cassiopeia, the Pleiades, Corvis."

retina of the eye views these elements individually."

"Oh," said Eric doubtfully. In an attempt to keep up his end of the conversation, he added, "It's small."

"Not as impressive as the photographs, I'll admit, although your binoculars give quite a good view."

"That thing with the photographs! Tell me how did you did that!" Eric demanded, lowering the binoculars.

"Merely a little magic trick. A magician never divulges his secrets."

"A magician! I thought you said you were an astronomer!"

The Professor was laughing again, louder and longer than before. Somehow, when his face was all smiles like it was now, he wasn't so scary. No, not scary at all. In fact, at this moment he looked quite friendly.

"I'm sorry. My intention was not to frighten you. Only to make you curious," he replied. "I see I was successful, however most of my guests come by the front way."

It was Eric's turn to be apologetic. "I know. I shouldn't have been spying on you. I'm sorry, too." Digging the toe of his tennis shoe in the rich black garden dirt, he asked quietly, "Um, Professor? Could I ask you something?"

Professor Strang said nothing.

Eric interpreted his silence as a positive response and continued, "Why choose me? I mean, I can understand why you'd pick Meredith. She's crazy about all this Astronomy stuff. But I've never really been interested in space."

The Professor remained silent for so long that Eric was afraid he had hurt his feelings. Then he answered in the same quiet voice Eric had used, "You're interested now, aren't you?"

"Yeah, I guess I am," Eric laughed. The Professor chuckled, too.

"Well, let's just say that I couldn't let all this equipment go to waste, and call it good, shall we?"

"Equipment?" asked Eric eagerly.

The Professor pointed to the tower behind them that Eric had noticed from the back of the house. "Yes. I have a telescope. It's quite nice. Would you like to see it?"

"Would I? More than anything, but . . . my Mom would kill me if I went into some strange guy's house."

"We can't have that now, can we? Wait here." The Professor disappeared into his house. A moment later, he reappeared, carrying two envelopes. Eric could barely make out what was written on them in the dim light. One of them was addressed to his mother, and the other was to the Weatherford's.

"What are these?" he asked.

"Consider them your passports to adventure."

"Huh?" The boy regarded the papers suspiciously. Although the Professor had ceased to frighten Eric, he had not lost his ability to confuse and bewilder.

"These are letters of introduction. Have Mr. Kincaid sign them. I believe your parents will trust your teacher's judgment."

"It's just my mom and me," Eric said quietly.

"Oh, well, that's fine. Then when she and Miss Weatherford's parents have signed them you both will be able to visit my observatory."

"Really? That would be awesome!"

The Professor seemed lost in thought for a time, gazing at the far away stars. Then he smiled. "I believe it will be a fascinating experience for all of us. Shall we begin a week from now, Friday evening at 7:00 pm?"

Eric nodded.

"Well then, off you go home before your mother becomes concerned."

Before Eric could think of anything else to say, the Professor was gone. Suddenly, the cold that he had previously been able to ignore was seeping through his thin jacket. As he turned to leave, a thought struck him. How had the Professor known to write those letters? Walking slowly, Eric looked up toward the tower. In the side of the dome facing him a dim, eerie, red light glowed through a tall, thin window. Eric thought he saw a figure standing there, watching him. He considered using the binoculars in order to be sure, but did not wish to be caught spying a second time. He turned and hurried away, more curious than ever about his new friend.

Chapter 4

Eric arrived at his house only ten minutes before his mom walked in the door. He had meant to call Meredith right away, but he was home later than he'd expected and the call would have to wait. He set his letter on the counter near the phone, and put Meredith's away in his backpack. Setting the oven to preheat, he opened the freezer and took out their usual Friday night pizza. He heard the door open behind him.

"Hi Mom, how was your meeting?" He turned to greet her.

"It was fine. It ran a little long, though. Thanks for putting dinner in. Again." She picked up his jacket from the chair where he'd thrown it and gave him that look that mothers give you. "Did you just get home?"

"Sorry, Mom." He evaded her question. "I was working on some stuff for school." He took the jacket and hung it up in the hall closet, and then returned to the kitchen. He set plates on the table and poured them each a glass of cola.

"How was school today?" She sat in one of the comfortable kitchen chairs. Eric sat opposite her. He enjoyed this part of their daily routine. They would usually sit like this each evening and talk about their day. All the way home he had been working out exactly what he would tell her.

"Mom, I met this really neat guy today. I mean, I actually met him on Wednesday, at Career Day. He's the Professor, you know, the Astronomy guy I told you about. I saw him again today. He has this observatory in his house and he wants Meredith and me to come and look through his big telescope." Eric supplied enough details so that he wouldn't feel guilty about not telling her everything. It didn't work. He still felt bad.

"Wow, you're excited! I thought Meredith was the one who was interested in Astronomy."

"Well, yeah. She is. She got invited, too." He showed her the envelope. She opened it and read the letter.

When she had finished, she looked up and said, "Sounds great! Is this something you'd really like to do?"

"Yeah, Mom. Meredith and I both want to." Eric crossed his fingers, hoping that the Weatherford's would agree to sign *her* letter.

"So what's the Professor like?" she asked.

Eric described him to her, leaving out any detail he could think of that might make the Professor seem strange or dangerous. Unfortunately, that didn't leave very much to tell. Once again, he felt a pang of guilt for not describing all the weird things that had happened since Wednesday. He knew if he did though, that his chances of seeing the inside of that observatory were zero.

"Okay. Take it to Mr. Kincaid on Monday and get him to sign it. In the meantime, I'll check out a few of these references. I have a long lunch on Wednesday. I'll call this Professor of yours and arrange to meet him and then you can go. After your homework is done, of course."

That had been a lot easier than Eric had expected! He hoped that Meredith would have good luck with her parents. Even now, Eric wasn't sure he wanted to go into the Professor's house alone. He seemed nice enough, but it was hard to forget how uneasy they'd felt that day at school.

"Is it okay if I call Meredith?" Eric quickly cleared the table and put the dishes in the dishwasher.

"Sure, dear. But would you use the upstairs phone? I have some work to do in my office."

Eric hurried up the stairs. He dialed Meredith's number and let it ring several times. When the message machine clicked on he hung up, frustrated. Then he remembered that Meredith was going to her grandmother's for dinner. He would just have to wait. He paced his room a few times. He had never been very good at waiting. Luckily, only a few minutes had passed before the phone rang.

"So, what happened?" Meredith barely gave him a chance to pick up the phone. "Did you go over there?"

Even though his embarrassment about spying on the Professor still lingered, Eric described the entire evening from the moment he left the house until he arrived home an hour and a half later.

"So as soon as we get these papers signed we'll be able to look through the telescope," explained Eric.

"Well . . . I don't know. You know how overboard my parents go making sure everything's safe. Remember the camping trip last year?"

Eric remembered. He and Meredith had been asked by one of their classmates to go on a youth group camping trip last summer. Her parents had almost messed up the whole thing because they were worried about who was driving, whether they had enough life jackets along, and a hundred other things. In the end she still got to go, but it was iffy there for a while.

"Besides," continued Meredith, "are you really planning to go inside his house? Have you forgotten that whole thing at school, with the pictures and the cards in our mailboxes–." She hummed the theme song from *The Twilight Zone.*

Eric wished at that moment that Meredith had been with him that evening. It was impossible to explain to her how in one quick instant he could go from being afraid of the Professor to not being afraid of him. All you had to do was sit there and look at the stars, and hear his quiet voice, and you knew that he was all right. She would just have to trust him.

"You're the one who said all that spinning stuff was just some kind of a trick. You're the Astronomy expert!" he sputtered. "You should be jumping at the chance to go see this guy's telescope!"

"Yeah, but that doesn't mean I'm going to do something stupid," she said, her feelings hurt.

"It's not stupid! If you don't want to go, just say so!" Eric knew that Meredith was upset because he had gone to the Professor's house without her. What Meredith did not tell him, was that she was sure her parents would never let her go to that observatory. And she *did* want to go with him – more than anything! She knew that when it came right down to it, she would be willing to overcome any obstacle in order to look through that big telescope, even her uncertainty about the Professor.

"Of course I want to go. I'll work it out somehow," she said.

* * * * * * *

Meredith soon found that getting her parents to sign that form was even harder than she thought it would be. Her father had been suspicious since the moment he'd found the Professor's card in their mailbox last Wednesday. She had tried to explain it away, saying that perhaps it was an advertisement for a class or something. Unfortunately, her dad didn't buy that, which made it even more difficult to figure out what to tell him when she gave him the letter to sign. They discussed it almost every night that week, and their conversations always seemed to go the same way.

"When did you meet this Professor, dear? Eat your potatoes, Katie." Her mother was an expert at carrying on two conversations at one time. They were at dinner and as usual, her little sister Katie was playing with her food.

"Why do you want to do telescope stuff, anyway?" asked her sister as she made a mountain out of her mashed potatoes. "Telescopes are for boys. How come you don't stay home and play with me?"

Meredith ignored her. "I told you about him, Mom. It was last week. You know, we had Career Day at school. I went to the session they had on Astronomy, and Professor Strang was there."

"And you think that this Professor put that business card in our mailbox to drum up interest in some class he is planning? Why didn't he just print out a flyer or something?" asked her dad.

"I don't really know, Dad." Meredith was frustrated. This was Tuesday already, and she still had not been able to get her parents to be reasonable. "All I know is that he invited Eric and me to come see his observatory because he knew we'd be interested. I'm sure he's okay, Dad. Mr. Kincaid knows him, after all."

"That's true, dear," her mother said. "Mr. Kincaid wouldn't have recommended the man if he didn't trust him." Meredith smiled gratefully at her mom, who for the first time seemed to be on her side. Maybe she was finally wearing down. Dad, on the other hand, was nowhere close to giving in.

"Well," he sighed, "maybe I'll get a chance to check out some of these references next week some time."

"Next week! Dad! Eric's mom already said he could go!"

"Don't shout at me, young lady. I'm sure Mrs. Spencer knows what she's doing," he said. "And I'm also sure that you are not going over to that man's house until I've met him and checked into his background. I'm not taking any chances with my little girl."

Meredith's heart sank. Knowing her dad, with his methodical engineer's mind, this was going to take forever. But she buried her frustration and forced herself to be agreeable.

"I'm sorry, Dad. It's just that Eric is going over to the Professor's on Friday and I wanted to be able to go with him. I'll bet they're going to look at Andromeda and M-13; all sorts of great stuff."

"Hmm. We'll see. In the meantime, why don't you help your mom clear the table?"

"Can I go see the telescope, too?" Katie had apparently forgotten that telescopes were for boys and she looked up hopefully at her older sister.

"No, Squirt." Meredith answered.

"Why not?"

"Because you aren't old enough. And besides, you weren't invited."

* * * * * * *

An entire week had gone by. Eric's form lay signed and ready on his desk next to the card with Professor Strang's name and address on it. He had hoped that by Friday the Weatherford's would have finally decided that the Professor was not a mass murderer. He also hoped that with the weekend ahead, his mother would not find any extra chores for him to do.

He picked up the card and re-read the motto printed on it. 'You're always safe with the Professor.' Too bad Meredith's parents couldn't just take what the card said on faith.

Meredith had told him not to wait any longer. Disappointment and excitement were warring within him. He really had wanted her to go with him. As hard as he tried, he could not avoid thinking about all the scary feelings the Professor had awakened in him that day at school. Having Meredith along would have gone a long way toward making him feel more comfortable about spending an evening with the unusual man. On the other hand, sitting outside his house that night, looking at the stars, Eric had gotten the sense that there was nothing to fear. He was sure that the card told the truth. So, here he was with his backpack over his shoulder and the letter in his hand. He was going.

It was still light out as he waved goodbye to his mother. It had been a major surprise to him that she was letting him go alone this first night, but she had been so impressed after visiting the Professor and seeing his observatory that she had actually encouraged him to go. They had agreed that he would telephone once he had reached the Professor's house and that she would pick him up at 11:00. He reassured her that he was perfectly able to walk the short distance home, but here Mom drew the line.

"Don't push your luck," was her comment.

When he reached the address on Mountain Lane, the pink and orange colored twilight had nearly faded from the western sky, and he was surprised once again to notice that, with the exception of the small red rectangle in the tower, there was not a light showing in any window of the house. That's funny, Eric thought. Doesn't he ever turn on any lights? In Biology class he had heard about people who were photophobic and spent their entire lives in darkened rooms, but that couldn't possibly apply to the Professor. After all, that day in the classroom he had stood at the chalkboard with the full light of the sun gleaming from his white lab coat. No, that couldn't be the explanation.

As Eric approached the door, it opened before he could locate the doorbell or knock. From out of the darkness came a voice.

"Good evening, Mr. Spencer. I see you've found the front door!"

Chapter 5

"If you don't mind my asking, why do you keep it so dark?" Eric's voice sounded loud in his own ears. The Professor had closed the door behind them and was now leading him through what Eric supposed was the living room of the large house.

"Dark adaptation occurs when the pupil of the eye opens to about 7 millimeters, allowing more light to reach the retina," explained the Professor. "This process takes approximately 30 minutes. If full dark adaptation is to be maintained, the eye must not be subjected to any form of white light, as that will cause the pupil to narrow again. Then the entire process of dilation would have to be repeated."

Eric's heart sank. Without Meredith with me, I'm way out of my league.

"Um, sir? Was that English you were speaking?"

"Good night vision is essential for viewing deep sky objects through a telescope," laughed the Professor. "The electric lights that we use to light our homes and streets make it difficult for our eyes to adjust to the darkness quickly. Submariners and airline pilots learned long ago that using red tinted lights would allow them to read maps and charts without spoiling their night vision."

That's better, thought Eric. And that explains the weird red glow I saw through the upstairs window the other night, too. Remembering that he had promised to call his mother, he looked around for a telephone.

"Professor Strang, could I use your –"

"Telephone? Certainly." The Professor picked up a cell phone and handed it to him. "Help yourself."

He always seems to know what I'm going to say before I say it, thought Eric. He called his mother and reassured her that he had arrived safely. She reminded him that, as agreed, she would be waiting for him in front of the address he had given her at 11:00.

"Okay, we're all set!" Eric handed the cell phone back to the Professor.

Tonight, the man was dressed all in black; black slacks, black shirt, black sweater. Eric nearly lost sight of him completely as they began to climb a narrow flight of stairs. Professor Strang's voice seemed to hang in the air ahead of them. It gave Eric the uncomfortable feeling that he was in the company of a disembodied spirit. He tried to shake off the image. At this point, Eric would have welcomed Meredith's glow-in-the-dark Einstein shirt!

Almost as if he *were* a mind reader, the Professor said, "I know it must be unnerving, walking around in the darkness in a strange person's home. You'll get used to it." A chuckle floated in the dim air. "Ah, here we are." Eric heard a door open and suddenly the staircase was flooded with a ghostly red light.

"This is the observatory," the Professor said with a hint of pride in his voice.

Eric did not want to hurt the man's feelings, but from what he could make out in the dim light there was nothing much to be impressed about. The space did look much larger than it had seemed from outside, but that was the only unusual thing about it. Surprised at how cold the room was compared to the remainder of the house, he quickly slipped his coat back on.

"Gosh, it's really cold-." His words died on his lips as the Professor pointed upward. The first stars of the evening winked at him brightly. There was no ceiling! And no roof either! Instead the room was covered by a gigantic white dome. An eight foot gap split the dome from side to side, so that the room lay open to the night sky.

"Wow! This is awesome!"

Stepping further into the room, Eric saw something even more amazing. Taking up almost the entire center of the observatory was the most unusual telescope he'd ever seen.

It was perched on a massive cylinder that was anchored to the floor and rose shiny and sleek toward the sky. Great arms cradled it upon a smaller central pedestal which housed a control center that looked as if it had come straight out of a science fiction novel. Its lines were clean and polished; no sign of cables or cords, knobs or gears marred it futuristic surface.

"This is the Discovery VII Telescope, the only one of its kind in existence." Now the pride in the Professor's voice was unmistakable.

As the boy moved closer, he was overwhelmed by the sheer size of the telescope. On his left a metal stairway led to a platform upon which two or three people could stand at one time, making the lower end of the giant tube accessible. Eric slowly climbed the ladder, reached out, and with the Professor's nod of permission, laid his hand on the base of the telescope.

"Meredith should be here to see this," he said regretfully.

"Don't worry, Eric. She will," Professor Strang assured him. "What would you like to look at first?"

"Saturn!" said Eric without consideration.

"Rotate to 175 degrees," the Professor commanded.

Suddenly Eric was jerked off his feet. Earthquake! He stumbled to his left, but the platform railing kept him from falling.

"Easy, Eric. Hold on," said the Professor. He rested a reassuring hand on the boy's arm. Eric struggled to regain his footing. Wait a minute, he thought. It's not an earthquake. The whole room is turning!

"What's happening?" To his embarrassment, Eric's voice shook slightly.

"An observatory wouldn't be very effective if it always faced in the same direction," explained the Professor. "Look!"

He pointed toward the open sky that was visible through the gap in the dome. A panorama of stars wheeled above them in a sky that had now become completely dark. A portion of one of the star shapes that Professor Strang had

"This is the Discovery VII Telescope, the only one of it's kind...."

shown him from the garden last week drifted lazily into view and then was gone again.

Just as suddenly and mysteriously as it had begun, the movement stopped.

"How did you do that?" Eric asked.

"The observatory dome rests in a circular channel mounted –"

"You're doing it again," Eric complained.

"Pardon me?"

"You're doing it again. You know, the foreign language thing."

"Oh, sorry." The Professor shrugged and offered what he hoped was a more acceptable answer. "Ball bearings?"

"Thank you." Eric's tone of voice got his meaning across clearly. Why didn't you say that in the first place? "And you just talk to the room and it moves?"

"Not the entire room, actually. Only the dome, the telescope itself, and the platform upon which we are standing. They are controlled by the computer, and the computer is voice activated."

"Controlled by you?"

"Yes."

"Oh." Even the man's simple explanations were more than he could understand at times. Eric stood by his side and was content to watch for the moment. It was silent for some time, but just as Eric began to wonder if he had been forgotten the Professor turned from the shiny body of the telescope and motioned for Eric to take his place.

"Look here."

Eric put his eye to the place where he had seen the Professor looking. It was like looking through one lens of an oversized pair of binoculars. He saw a large, very bright point of light with two small lines crossed directly over the center of it.

"Hey, this is like looking through my dad's hunting rifle scope," said Eric.

"It's built on the same principle, basically. You are looking at a portion of the constellation Taurus. We locate this area in the Discovery's finder scope, and then with a few minor adjustments . . .," the Professor looked through another eyepiece which was centered in the base of the brass tube. With his right hand he adjusted the focusing ring. "There we are."

Stepping forward, Eric situated himself so that he could look through the telescope as the Professor had instructed him.

"Now, move your head slightly from side to side until the image comes into view."

At first he saw nothing, but as Eric did as he was told, he found what he was searching for. He gasped in delight, for there hung Saturn in its ringed splendor. The separate rings could be seen clearly, with the blackness of space showing in between. Although the colors were not as intense as those he had seen in the photographs at school, they were still present in a variety of shades of orange, yellow, and red. Resting inside the rings, the planet's disc was a little smaller than the size of a quarter.

"What's that spot?" Eric's voice was muffled as he continued looking through the eyepiece.

"Lower left quadrant, near the ring's edge?" asked the Professor. "That, my friend, is Titan, one of Saturn's many moons."

"Saturn has more than one moon?"

"Yes, indeed. I believe the count now stands at 32. Only a few are visible with this equipment, however."

"Wow! That's a lot! Why is it so bright? It's not a star, is it? Like the sun?" he asked.

"No, Saturn is a planet, although it does possess some of a star's ingredients – hydrogen, helium, among others. These ingredients are responsible for the planet's colors. The brilliance, in this case, is reflected sunlight." He tapped Eric gently on the shoulder to get his attention.

"You see, here we are on the planet Earth." Professor Strang stepped over to the computer console and picked up several spheres of different sizes. He held up a small, dark ball and plopped it into Eric's outstretched hand. "This," the Professor held up a larger ball, "is Sol, our sun. And this," he presented a third ball, "is Saturn. Follow me."

The Professor lead the way down the ladder and over to a long worktable at the other side of the room. "Desk lamp, on." He spoke quietly to the air. Miraculously it seemed, a small desk lamp blinked on. Surprised and nearly blinded by the sudden brightness, Eric covered his eyes.

"Hey! Won't this white light ruin our night vision?" he asked.

"Very good, Mr. Spencer. But the light is necessary for this demonstration, and our eyes will quickly adapt once we are finished." He reached out and took Eric's hand that still held the 'Earth' and raised it up to eye level. Eric could now see that the ball was mottled blue and green.

"Earth is approximately 150 million kilometers; 93 million miles from the sun." He put the large yellow globe on a shelf behind the lamp on the table, and then returned to where Eric was standing. One side of the ball Eric was holding was bright with lamp light. The Professor pointed to the darkened side.

"Right now, we are on the night side of our Earth, the side which faces away from the sun. Saturn is here, 800 million miles farther out into space, give or take a few million miles." As he spoke, he took several large steps into the dimness of the room and held up the ball that represented the ringed planet. As he moved away, Eric could see that the side of the ball facing him was still shining brightly.

"So you can see," continued the Professor, "that only a portion of the light from the sun hits Earth. The rest of Sol's light shines out into space and is reflected back by other objects in the near vicinity."

"Near? I thought you said that Saturn was millions of miles away from us," said Eric.

Professor Strang smiled, pleased at his newest student's quick-mindedness. "Near and far are relative terms, Eric. When most distances across space are measured in light years, a few million miles are only a drop in the interstellar bucket, so to speak." He collected the three spheres and then to the boy's delight began to juggle them in the air.

"Desk lamp off." The room became dark once more as the computer complied. "Shall we return to our viewing?" asked the Professor.

This guy is still full of surprises, thought Eric, and followed his new mentor back up the ladder.

Chapter 6

"It's not fair!" Meredith shouted. "Why do I have to watch Katie tonight?"

"Dear, you know that Daddy and I have had tickets to this play for weeks," answered Mrs. Weatherford. "I told you several days ago that we needed you to watch your sister. Why are you making such a fuss about it?"

"Because tonight is the night that Eric is going over to Professor Strang's house to look through his telescope. We were both invited and I really wanted to go." Meredith couldn't believe that her mother didn't remember something that was so important to her.

"Well, Meredith, you're just going to have to go some other time, that's all. Your father hasn't had a chance to meet Professor Strang yet. Now, make sure that you and Katie have your dinner and after you put the dishes away would you take Sandy out for a walk? Then you can watch a movie or read to your sister. She can stay up 'til 9:00 or so."

"All right, Mom." Meredith's voice was filled with disappointment.

"I'm sorry, honey. Daddy's calling me and I have to go." Mrs. Weatherford picked up her coat and headed out the door. "Lock up behind me and, dear, do try to stand up straight! Being tall is not a crime, you know."

"Yes, Mom."

As soon as the door closed behind her mother, Meredith plopped down on the couch next to her sister. Katie was glued to the T.V., watching one of her favorite shows, and hardly noticed her. Meredith was glad. She wanted to think, and if Katie got into one of her ask-a-million-questions moods, thinking would be impossible.

She hoped that Katie had not overheard her talking to Mom. Her feelings might have been hurt. Usually Meredith enjoyed spending time with her sister and didn't mind the occasional baby sitting job. All she could think about tonight, though, was that Eric was at the observatory and she wasn't.

"Dog-gone it, it's just not fair!" she moaned again. As if in response, the Weatherford's golden retriever came bouncing into the room. Tail wagging, he jumped up into Meredith's lap and began to lick her with his drippy, wet tongue.

"I didn't mean you, you big dufus! Get down, Sandy!" Meredith pushed the big dog away and stood up. Sandy tried again with Katie, lapping sloppily at her face. Without taking her eyes from her program, Katie patted the couch where her sister had been sitting moments before. Sandy accepted the invitation and made himself comfortable.

Brushing the dog's hair from her jeans, Meredith went to the kitchen where she washed her hands and began to prepare dinner for the two of them. While the meatloaf her mom had made was warming in the microwave, she fed Sandy. As she was dishing up a generous portion of food for the dog, her eyes fell on his harness and leash hanging on the back porch.

A slow smile spread across her face. They don't call me brilliant for nothing, thought Meredith.

"Come get your dinner, Katie. And then we're going to take Sandy for a walk."

Katie sighed. Meredith wasn't sure if she was upset about not getting to finish her T.V. show or because she didn't want to go for a walk, but at this point she didn't care. All that mattered was that after dinner, the two of them were going to take a little stroll that would lead them right by Professor Strang's house.

Meredith hurried through her dinner, so that as soon as Katie was finished, she could whisk their plates and cups into the dishwasher. She grabbed a coat for herself and tossed Katie's across the room to her, encouraging her to zip up and put on some gloves.

"What's your hurry?" asked the little girl.

"Um, no hurry," answered Meredith. "I just want to get Sandy out for his walk. You know, before he has an accident."

"Sandy hasn't peed on the carpet since he was a puppy." Katie looked up at her sister suspiciously. There was something going on here that she couldn't quite figure out. Meredith usually had to be told twice to walk the dog. Now she was volunteering?

"Don't say pee," said Meredith, trying to change the subject. "It's gross. Besides, Mom doesn't like it."

"It's better than saying poop."

"Whatever." Meredith pulled Katie through the open doorway with one hand, and the dog with the other. At least I'm doing what Mom told me to do, but I don't think this is exactly what she had in mind, she thought with a pang of guilt as she locked the door behind her.

As they walked, Meredith let Katie keep up a running stream of conversation, hoping it would keep her mind off the direction they were taking. It wasn't the usual way they went when Sandy needed to stretch his legs. However, it wasn't very long before Katie stopped talking about her week at school and the Barbie doll party she was planning for her eighth birthday, and started looking around her.

"Hey!" she said. "This isn't the way we usually go!"

"Shh!" said Meredith. She wasn't exactly sure who would overhear them out here in the street, but she couldn't get over the feeling that she was doing something that her mom and dad would definitely not approve of and she didn't need her sister's pesky questions to remind her of that fact.

"Where are we going?" Katie continued.

"We're taking Sandy for a walk. It doesn't matter which way we go!" Sandy had stopped to sniff a patch of grass along the street, and Meredith jerked on his leash and told him to heel.

"Okay! You don't have to get mad!" Katie crossed her arms angrily and looked away, her lower lip sticking out in her usual pout. They walked on in silence for a few moments, before Katie realized that Meredith was no longer at her side. She turned around, dismayed to see how dark it had become. They had come to the dead end of a street that she was not familiar with. There were no street lights and no lights on the one lonely house that stood overlooking the edge of the bluff.

At the grown up age of seven, Katie did not like to admit that she was still afraid of the dark, so she quickly hurried back to her big sister's side. Meredith did not even seem to notice her, or the dog. She was standing in the middle of the empty street, gazing up at the house. Using a small flashlight she carried in her pocket, Meredith compared the words on a small card with the address on the house.

"What's that?" Katie made a grab for the card, but it was out of her reach. Meredith slid the card into the back pocket of her jeans, but not before Katie had seen what was printed on it.

"Hey, isn't this that Professor guy's house? The one with the telescope?' she asked.

Meredith nodded. She pointed to the dome that stood high over one end of the house. "That's the observatory, right there. That's where the telescope is."

"What are *we* doing here? Mom and Dad are gonna be so mad at you! You'll get grounded for the rest of your life!" Now Katie was whispering.

"Be quiet! Mom and Dad aren't even going to know we were here, unless you open your big mouth and tell them!" As she was saying this, Meredith was doing some fast thinking. Katie had an excellent point. If I go in there now, without Dad's permission, he'll never sign that paper. Then I'll never get to look through the telescope. What was I thinking? On the other hand, Eric was probably inside right now with the Professor, looking through his telescope. I'm the one who should be in there, she thought. I'm the one who likes planets and stars, not Eric!

With a heavy sigh of frustration, Meredith let her gaze drift upward. Above the trees, above the Professor's house, millions of stars winked back at her from the dark night sky. Despite her annoyance at the situation, the sight had the usual effect of calming her down. What a fantastic view!

"Can we go home now?" Katie whined. She was feeling totally ignored. "I'm freezing!"

"Just a minute. I guess it won't hurt anything if I just knock on the door and say 'hello'. Here." She shoved Sandy's leash into her little sister's hand and marched toward the front door of the house with a determined look on her face.

Just then Sandy, who until now had been content to sit beside them, leapt to his feet and began barking furiously. Before Meredith could grab his harness, the dog had jerked his leash from Katie's small hand and bolted down the street, back the way they had come. The two sisters dashed after him at top speed calling his name loudly, but Sandy quickly disappeared into the darkness.

* * * * * * *

"Hey, where'd it go?" Eric turned away from the eyepiece to look back at the Professor.

"What is it you've lost?"

"Well, Saturn, actually. It was right there, before. And now it's gone! Did the telescope get moved?" asked Eric; more than half afraid he'd done something wrong.

"No, the earth did," answered the Professor.

"What-?"

"I'm sure you remember from your science classes at school that the earth rotates on its axis, correct?"

Eric nodded.

"Stand up, boy. No, turn around, but keep your eyes on me."

The Professor motioned for Eric to spin in place. As he turned, it dawned on him what Professor Strang was getting at. "I see. I'm the earth, you're the stars. Right?"

"Right you are. And as the earth turns, the stars move across your field of view. During the time we were

"Can we go home now?" Katie whined. "I'm freezing!"

performing our little experiment, the earth turned nearly four degrees on its axis. Saturn is now," he looked through the eyepiece and made a slight adjustment, "right there!" He backed away so Eric could return to his viewing place.

"Thanks." At first, the image appeared washed out, lighter in color than it had been before. The Professor explained that this was the result of the bright light they had used for their experiment a few moments ago. Once Eric's eyes had become adapted to the room's darkness, the colors would reappear. In addition, Eric noticed that the longer he gazed at the image, the more colorful it became.

"Your eyes are behaving in much the same way as the telescope, gathering light and reflecting it. The more light the retina gathers, the more colorful the image. Understand?"

"Yes. And I didn't even have to ask for a translation. Either I'm beginning to think like you, or you're beginning to talk like me. I'm not sure which worries me more."

The Professor laughed. He was glad the boy was beginning to feel more at ease in his presence. Eric, on the other hand, was amazed at himself. He had never imagined that he would ever feel comfortable enough with this man to joke around with him, let alone after spending only one evening in his company.

"Do you have to keep adjusting the telescope so that it will keep pointing at what you want to see?" asked Eric.

"Well, yes. That's one way of doing it. Or you can engage the clock drive." Before Eric had a chance to inquire, the Professor volunteered an explanation. "It's a device that is attached to the computer that compensates for Earth's rotation. As the planet turns, the telescope moves with the precision of a clock, keeping the object you are centered on within the field of view."

"That's neat."

"Very neat. Are you ready to look at something else?" asked the Professor.

"Sure thing!" Eric responded.

For the next hour or so, the astronomer and his new apprentice explored the universe together. With very little explanation, the Professor patiently located one celestial object after another for the boy to enjoy.

"I call this 'playing tourist'," said Professor Strang. "It's like a sight seeing trip to the stars."

By now, Eric had become used to the platform moving on its own under his feet and the ceiling rotating above his head, although none of the movements the observatory had made were as violent as that first one. He was beginning to suspect that the Professor had surprised him like that on purpose. In fact, thought Eric, I'll bet that's the reason behind a lot of his strange behavior. He wants me to think he's this mysterious wizard who can perform magic or something. Who's kidding who, Eric laughed to himself. That's exactly what I thought!

The observatory was stationary again, and Professor Strang had finished making adjustments to the telescope before descending the ladder and crossing the room to the main computer control system. Right now, the Discovery was centered on Andromeda, he explained, a spiral galaxy that is located 2.26 million light years from Earth.

Eric was forced to stoop quite low in order to look through the telescope in its present position. For a moment he lost his balance, and without taking his eyes from the fascinating image of the galaxy that was now in view, he reached out to steady himself against the base of the telescope. Suddenly he became dizzy, and at the same time he felt a sickening stretching sensation in the pit of his stomach. He lost the sense of looking through an eyepiece and as he stepped back, he realized that the telescope was no longer there. The observatory was gone as well, and the galaxy, which only a moment before had been the size and shape of a half dollar on its side, was now a gigantic wheel of blinding, multi-colored light. No barrier that he could see stood between himself and the mighty cosmic wheel, and terror gripped him as he felt himself falling directly into its swirling center.

Before he could draw a breath to scream, Eric again felt ill. He closed his eyes for a moment, and when he opened them the galaxy had returned to its previous size. He could feel the hard metal of the platform under his feet. In the pale dim glow of red light, Eric could see that the Professor was still at his desk with his back turned as though nothing at all had happened. The room was cold and quiet, exactly as he had left it.

Left it?! Eric frantically groped for an explanation of what he had just experienced.

"Um, Professor?" Eric's voice came out sounding strange and weak.

"Yes?" answered the Professor calmly. His eyes did not leave the page upon which he was writing.

Eric's mouth moved, but no words came out. He could not think of a single thing to say that wouldn't sound totally crazy. All the wonder, the curiosity and yes, the fear he had experienced upon first meeting the Professor had returned in full force. His arms and legs were paralyzed, as were his thoughts. If the room had caught on fire at that moment he could not have escaped.

"What is it, Eric?" The Professor turned now to look at the boy.

"I – I – ," Eric searched for something to say to fill the dark silence. "I think it's time for me to go." Eric was anxious to put as much distance between himself and this incredible situation as possible. He needed time to think, time to figure out what was going on.

The Professor crossed to the window. "Yes, your mother is waiting with the car. Would she like to come in and visit for a moment?"

Eric was caught off guard by the Professor's manner. He was acting as though he had no idea that his student had just taken an unplanned trip to the far stars and back! He seemed not to notice that Eric was so confused and flustered that he could barely put a sentence together.

"Ah, no thanks. I think - she probably wants to go right home." Eric was edging his way toward the door, trying to keep as far away from the Professor as he could.

"Well then, young man. I hope you enjoyed the viewing this evening. Shall we agree to meet again one week from tonight? Perhaps Miss Weatherford will be allowed to join us."

"Yeah, sure." As much as Eric wanted to get out of there, he was reluctant to leave without some sort of reasonable explanation. He was badly frightened, but he still couldn't help feeling that there was nothing dangerous about this man or his motives. When he reached the door of the observatory, Eric turned back and said, "Um, Professor Strang?"

"Yes?"

"Thanks for letting me use your telescope. I had a really great time."

He took the stairs two at a time. As he reached the main floor, he could hear the Professor's deep laughter. It followed him all the way out the door.

Chapter 7

"You're awfully quiet tonight," said Eric's mother. "You hardly said a word in the car on the way home. Are you feeling all right?"

"Yeah, Mom. My head hurts, that's all." Eric was lying on the couch, staring up at the ceiling. "Too much excitement, I guess."

"Well, it's late. Why don't I give you something for it and then you can go on up to bed. A good night's sleep fixes a lot of things. "

"Sure, Mom." Like I'm going to be able to sleep, thought Eric. Before he went upstairs to his room, he gave his mother a quick hug. "Thanks for letting me go tonight. It was really fun."

Surprised at the unusual show of affection, Mrs. Spencer returned the hug and then ran her hands through her son's hair. It's about time for a haircut, she thought. She watched as Eric climbed the stairs. She was a little worried about him. Something was bothering the boy, and she knew from past experience that it was not easy for Eric to share certain things with her. She wished for the millionth time that his father were here to help him through these next few years. Being a teenager was hard enough when you had two parents.

Eric quickly changed into his pajamas, which consisted of a pair of shorts and an old T-shirt. He was not really tired, but he lay down on his bed anyway to see if he could get rid of this annoying headache. Besides, if his mom heard him roaming around in his room she would be up here in a minute, checking on him. Her concern both pleased and embarrassed him. He wondered if all mothers were the same, or if his mom treated him the way she did because he no longer had a dad.

What he really needed was to talk to Meredith. He hoped she would be home in the morning. There was so much to tell her, Eric hardly knew where to start. I suppose I can just say that I got sucked through the Professor's telescope to the Whatchamacallit Galaxy, Eric thought, and see where the conversation goes from there. He did not have the slightest doubt that she would believe him. They were best friends, after all. He could tell her anything, no matter how far fetched. But if she thought she'd missed the astronomical event of the century, she might never speak to him again. Who would blame her? Maybe if she had been there, nothing out of the ordinary would have happened. Or better yet, thought Eric, maybe it would have happened to her!

He smiled to himself as he went over in his mind how he would tell her about the whole evening. He could hardly wait to see the look on her face. His smile widened as he pictured her taking her first look through the big scope and seeing all the planets and galaxies he had seen. Won't she be surprised when that telescope takes *her* to the -.

Geez! What am I saying? One minute the Professor and his telescope scare me out of my wits, he thought, and the next minute I'm so excited to look through that thing again I can hardly stand it. Eric could no longer lay still. He sat up on the side of his bed and turned on the light. Am I actually thinking about going back there?

Eric considered the question for a few moments. Professor Strang was definitely strange with an 'e', yet Eric knew instinctively that he had nothing to fear from the man. He wasn't sure if that was because of the words on the card, or because of the kind and gentle voice in which the Professor gave his instructions and explanations. Maybe it was a combination of the two, or something completely different that had not even occurred to him yet. All he knew was that he trusted the Professor. I even like the guy, he said to himself. Eric lay back on his pillows while he considered this surprising new thought. Yeah, I like him a lot.

And just how scary was it, really? After all, I didn't get hurt. I just felt a little dizzy, and then I was there and back again. No harm done. Maybe if I had asked the Professor about it instead of running off like I did, he would have explained everything to me. He told me about the pictures when I asked him, didn't he? Well, sort of, anyway. Eric realized that he wasn't being completely honest with himself; the Professor's explanation of those photographs had left a lot of unanswered questions.

Eric yawned. In the morning he would tell Meredith everything. Talking things over with his best friend always helped. He knew for certain now that when next Friday rolled around, he would again climb the stairs to the Professor's telescope. He smiled in anticipation and then sleep claimed him.

* * * * * * *

"Tell me all about it," Meredith pleaded. She had answered the phone on the first ring.

"Why don't you come over?" asked Eric. He would rather give her the details face to face.

"I can't. I'm grounded."

"Grounded! You're kidding me!" Eric couldn't believe his ears. "How could you possibly be grounded?" In the whole time he had been friends with Meredith, he had never known her to get into any trouble that was bad enough for her parents to ground her.

"It wasn't my fault!" she wailed. "Well, I mean, technically it was my fault that the dog got off his leash, but who would have known that he'd run off like that? Katie was supposed to-."

"Meredith!" Eric interrupted her. "Slow down and tell me what happened." He could tell she was upset and reasoned that she might be more willing to listen to him if he heard her out first.

"Okay. Last night I had to baby sit Katie, and I was really mad that I couldn't go to the Professor's house with you. So after we had dinner, I took Katie and Sandy out for a walk. Instead of going the way we usually go, you know, down by the park, we –," she hesitated. "-- we walked over to the Professor's house."

"The Professor's house! What time was that? I was probably there! I didn't see you. Why didn't you come in?"

Eric was thinking that if only she *had* been there, he wouldn't have to figure out a way to fill her in on the creepy details.

"I did try to ring the bell. But then Sandy got off his leash and started to bark at nothing, and ran off into the woods. It took me half an hour running around in the dark to finally catch him and drag him home."

"What did your parents say?"

"Well, at first they didn't say much of anything. They didn't know about it. But then Katie opened her big mouth and told the whole story to Mom and Dad. Well," she added with a sigh of relief, "not the whole story, thank goodness. If they knew I had been over to the Professor's house, I'd be grounded for a year instead of a week."

"How come Katie didn't tell them that part, too?" Eric asked.

"Because I bribed her!" Meredith explained. "Cost me all of last week's allowance. I'd have given her this week's too, except there won't be any. Loss of cash flow is Dad's way of showing his disapproval." Meredith had expected Eric to laugh at that remark, but the only response she heard was an impatient sigh, so she changed the subject.

"So never mind that. What was it like? What did you look at?" she asked.

Eric's willingness to let Meredith finish her story had given him more time to think. He had decided to start at the beginning and lead slowly up to the moment where things began to get weird. He described the Professor's house and the observatory, allowing Meredith to interrupt him occasionally to ask questions. He told her about the experiments that Professor Strang had used to explain to him about reflection and the movement of the earth. When he began to tell her how nice the Professor seemed and how much he had wished that she had been able to be there, he realized that he *was* stalling. He had to tell her now, or he would completely lose his nerve.

"Something strange happened." Eric said abruptly.

"Why does that not surprise me?" Meredith asked.

"After all, this *is* the Professor we're talking about. More abracadabra, right?"

"No, not exactly. Not like the photographs and stuff."

"Better than that?"

"I'm not sure I'd call it better, exactly. I – uh – I went somewhere." Eric swallowed hard. There, he'd said it.

"I know. You went to the Professor's house."

"No. I mean, I went somewhere after that."

"After that? You went home, didn't you?"

Eric shook his head and swallowed the large amount of moisture that seemed to be keeping his tongue from working correctly.

"I went to this galaxy we were looking at."

"You went to this galaxy?" Meredith's habit of repeating what she did not understand often became annoying. This was one of those times. "What galaxy? What was it called?"

"Who cares what it was called!"

"I do! You promised me you'd remember all the things you looked at and tell me their names. And now you can't even remember the name of the –"

Gee whiz, for someone that's so smart . . . Eric allowed the thought to fizzle out in frustration. "Considering what happened, I'm lucky I can remember my own name! Didn't you hear what I said? I traveled through the Professor's telescope to another gal-ax-y!" Maybe if I speak slowly enough she'll get it, he thought. Whispering now, so that his mom would not overhear him, Eric told her all about feeling dizzy and seeing the coin-sized image grow to gigantic dimensions.

"I was just hanging there in space. It was kind of like being inside of a fishbowl; everything was all wiggly and shimmery like when you open your eyes under water, you know? And then suddenly I felt something pulling me back."

Not a sound came from the other end of the phone. Eric was disappointed. He'd thought that Meredith would be as excited about his news as he was. By now she should be asking a few thousand questions.

"Well, aren't you going to say something?" he asked.

"Like what?" Judging by her tone of voice, Eric had a mental picture of her tossing back her long braids and shrugging her shoulders. "It was late. You must have fallen asleep and dreamed it all."

Eric thought seriously about this. At first, he had suggested the same thing to himself. But now that he heard Meredith say it out loud, he knew it was not the case. Even though it had seemed like a nightmare, he was sure that he had been completely awake.

"No! I wasn't asleep. It was real. Don't you think I'd know the difference?"

"Well, maybe. I just think you wanted something odd to happen. I mean, this guy pretends like he's some mysterious sorcerer and plays a few tricks on us. We let ourselves get all worried and scared over nothing. It was exhilarating for a while, and now you want to keep that adrenaline rush going. So you make up this preposterous story about space travel through a telescope, and expect me to buy it? Well I'm not that gullible!"

Eric couldn't believe what he was hearing. Meredith had been as alarmed by the Professor's behavior at their first meeting as he had been; just as stunned at the things they'd seen. She had been as determined as he to discover the reason why Professor Strang had chosen to leave his business card in their mailboxes. What was the matter with her all of a sudden?

"Wait, Meredith. We'll go back there together and you can see it for yourself!"

Meredith gave him no chance to say more. "Eric, it is absolutely impossible for a telescope to do what you say this one did. Telescopes are nothing more than a combination of mirrors that reflect light. They are not a means of transportation! And as for going with you, I – I'm not sure I even want to, now!"

"Meredith, you've just gotta believe me! I've never lied to you before. Why would I start now?"

"I have no idea. I have to go, Eric. I have things to do." Before he could say another word, she had slammed down the receiver.

On his end, Eric hung up slowly. What went wrong, he asked himself. Why wouldn't she listen to me? He wandered into the hallway, thinking over the entire conversation and wondering what he could have said differently. He suddenly realized that he was no longer bothered only by the prospect of not being believed. Something far worse had just occurred to him.

He had counted on Meredith's ability to find a rational explanation for everything that had happened to him at the Professor's place last night. She's the smartest person in the whole eighth grade, he thought. She's also the only person I can talk to about any of this. She has to help me! Eric was positive that the Professor intended him no harm, however he knew that a lot of that confidence had rested on the fact that when he returned to the observatory next week, Meredith would be going with him. But now he was totally alone!

His mother found him still standing there a few minutes later, his head hanging, completely unaware of her presence. She set down the basket of laundry she was carrying and watched him silently for a moment.

"Eric?"

The boy did not respond. He gave no sign that he had heard her at all.

"Eric, what's the matter?' Finally he turned toward her. She was shocked at his expression. His face was totally white, his eyes wide and staring. With a mother's instinct, she protectively wrapped both arms around him, drawing him close to her. She was relieved to feel him suddenly begin to hug her back.

"What is it, dear?" She led him over to the stairs and they sat down together on the top step. "Who was that on the phone?"

"It was Meredith." Eric's quiet voice reflected the misery he felt. "I – I called her to tell her all about last night. All of a sudden she got mad and said she had to go. Then she hung up."

"I don't understand, dear. Why was Meredith angry with you?" She still sat with her arm around his shoulders, a look of concern on her face. Eric felt some measure of comfort from her closeness.

"I'm not sure, Mom. She was really excited the other day when I told her I was going."

"Wasn't she supposed to go with you?"

"Yes. But her dad hadn't signed the permission form yet and besides, she had to baby sit on Friday night."

"Oh, I see. A double whammy! Meredith is probably just jealous that she had to miss it. After all, she is the one who has been interested in astronomy all these years. Try to put yourself in her shoes."

"What do you mean?" Eric asked.

"Well, try to see things from her point of view. How would it feel if for all your life you wanted to do something so very much, and then when the opportunity finally came, your best friend got to do it instead of you? Wouldn't you feel a bit angry and resentful, too?"

"I guess so." Eric thought about it awhile. "But it wasn't my fault. I wanted her to be there." More than anything, he thought.

"Sometimes we get so upset about our circumstances that some of the anger we feel spills over onto the people we love." She hugged him tightly again. "I was angry for a long time when your dad died," she added quietly.

"Angry at Dad?" Surprise at her statement caused Eric's eyebrows to nearly disappear into his hairline.

"Yes. Very angry."

"But why? Dad's accident wasn't his fault."

"I know. But I was angry with him anyway. For going to that teaching seminar. For leaving us alone. I was even angry at you for a time."

Eric didn't know what to say to that, so he remained silent, hoping his mother would explain. His eyes met hers and he was not surprised to see tears there.

"Caring for you and having to work at the same time; being here instead of our old home where all my friends were -- I was so frightened. You see? I wasn't really mad at you. How could I be?" She smiled and ruffled his hair. "I was just angry at the circumstances that life had handed me."

"Gosh, Mom, that must have been awful for you. I guess I was really selfish." He looked away, embarrassed.

"Oh, Eric, you weren't selfish, you were ten! I probably should have shared some of these feelings with you years ago, but I never seemed to be able to find the right opportunity." She put her hand on his shoulder. "Honey, look at me."

Eric turned to her, his blue eyes dark with emotion. "Why did he have to die, Mom? Why didn't he stay with us?"

"I don't know. I've asked myself that same question a million times. All I know is that your dad loved you. He loved being with you more than anything else in the world. He never would have left us, but he didn't have a choice. And we don't have a choice, either. He'll always be a part of our lives, but we have to go on without him, no matter how hard it seems."

She took a deep breath and let it out slowly. Pulling him closer to her, she said gently, "Now, about Meredith. Do you think if I call her parents and let them know that you came home in one piece from Dr. Strang's house, that maybe they'll let her go next time?"

"Gee, that would be great, Mom. Do you think they'll listen to you?" He gave her a small smile.

"I don't know, Eric. But it's worth a try." They both stood up. She picked up her laundry basket and as she walked past him into his room, he reached out and gave her another big hug. With the basket under one arm, she awkwardly returned it. "Hopefully," she said, "by next week things will all be back to normal."

"Gosh Mom, I guess I was really selfish."

Chapter 8

There was nothing normal about the week that followed. School went on as usual; except that in every class they shared Meredith avoided him completely. When she could not help speaking to him, her tone was cold and casual, as if she were addressing an utter stranger. Eric did not know what to do with himself. Since he had moved to Colorado Meredith had been his best friend. Even a few of the teachers noticed the stony silence between them and commented on it. Some of the students, who had long been envious of the close friendship between the two, were only too happy to make snide remarks to Eric as he made his way through the hallways. By Thursday he had heard quite enough.

"Where's your girlfriend, Eric?"

"Did the Human Encyclopedia finally dump ya for someone smart?"

It was after the seventh or eighth such remark that Eric quietly wished that he could just climb into his locker and stay there until the final bell rang. That actually wasn't such a bad idea, except that his teachers might notice his absence and call home. Going home now, that was a good idea, he thought. I could call Mom and tell her I don't feel good! Only then she'd have to leave work to come and get me and if she thought I was really sick, she wouldn't let me go tomorrow night.

Eric had gone over and over in his mind what to do about next Friday night. He had to accept Professor Strang's invitation to the observatory, or he'd go nuts wondering if his interstellar trip had been real or imaginary. He did not want to go again without Meredith, but maybe she had gotten her parents permission and would show up there in spite of what she'd said on the phone. On the other hand, if she was there and still mad at him, well, that could be a bit awkward. No one wanted to be around any girl when she was mad, especially Meredith. Her use of wit and words like bow and arrows was practically legendary. Eric was glad that so far, he had never been on the receiving end of her biting sarcasm.

Her fellow students were not that lucky. It was all Meredith could do to keep her temper amidst the same kinds of teasing that had dogged Eric's heels. It was in Math class that she could contain herself no longer.

"What possible difference could it make to you who my friends are?" she roared.

Eric watched her from across the classroom as she flung her long hair behind her and marched out the door, muttering. "I wonder if there's intelligent life on *other* planets!"

Way to go Meredith, thought Eric. He hurried after her. Maybe he could catch her between classes. If she was that mad at being made fun of she might be ready to patch things up. Or she might take it out on me, he thought, walking a little slower. He caught up with her just as she entered the Biology room and since they shared this period too, he followed her in. Eric had no intention of having it out with Meredith in front of his entire science class and since her face was still a thundercloud, he decided it might be safer to wait.

She took her seat and although her eyes never left the cover of her science book, she was aware of Eric as he crossed the room to his desk. Throughout the week she had found numerous ways to fuel her own anger, trying to convince herself how ridiculous Eric had been to expect her to believe him when obviously he had been making the whole thing up. Now, for the first time since last Friday, she had calmed down enough to see things more objectively. Maybe telling off those mathematical morons earlier was good medicine, she thought.

Fortunately Mr. Kincaid was giving them a study period today. She opened her book to the assigned pages, but while she only pretended to be reading, she mentally kicked herself for being the cause of this whole miserable week. If we were still friends, she thought, those vultures would never have started pecking at us in the first place. It's all my fault!

She had not failed to notice how well Eric had handled all of the awful teasing that he'd had to endure. She had to admit that from what she'd witnessed in the midst of pretending to ignore him, he had dealt with it much better than she had. She was really quite proud of him.

She put her head in her hands. With her eyes guarded as they were, she risked a look in Eric's direction. He was turned away from her, reading. Or pretending to read, she thought. I wonder if he's as unhappy as I am. One had only to look at the way he was sitting to have the answer to that question.

Meredith thought back to another time and another place, when she remembered Eric sitting in much the same way as he was now. Her view of the Biology class melted away and in her mind's eye, was replaced with another, smaller classroom. Eric was seated at another desk, similar to the way he sat now.

It was in the middle of their fifth grade year. Eric had been out of school the week before, because his father had died. She and her classmates did not really understand much about it. They were told that there had been an accident and that it was a hard time for Eric. They should give him some time to adjust.

That adjustment took a while longer than some of the kids were willing to wait. He had only been at their school since the beginning of the year, so he'd not had time to make many friends. She guessed that some of the kids just didn't want to be around someone who was sad all the time. It didn't bother her any. She liked Eric all the more because of the way he had managed his terrible loss. As hard as she tried sometimes, she couldn't imagine how awful it would be to lose a parent. She had spent a lot of time that year, trying to think of ways to make her friend's life a little happier. From that moment on there had never been a bit of trouble between them.

Until now, she thought. She was surprised to notice her eyes were wet with tears. She had not cried for him in that long ago time; why was she weeping for him now? What's wrong with me?

I'm not really mad at Eric, at least not anymore. She admitted to herself that when she had stood outside the Professor's house that night she'd felt the first cold fingers of anger stir within her. When Eric called her on Saturday morning and had begun to describe how the telescope looked and how it worked, how nice the Professor was and how carefully he had explained things, the coldness had blossomed into icy hands of jealousy that squeezed her heart like a vice. She could stand only so much of Eric's bragging!

Now that she thought about it though, she realized that bragging just wasn't Eric's style. He'd never been one who had too high an opinion of himself. In fact on many occasions, she'd needed to encourage her friend to have some confidence. Between the two of them, she had always been the more positive one.

Meredith turned the page of her science book to keep up the illusion that she was reading, and sighed. She was not used to examining her feelings in this way. She'd never had any reason to. Most of her relationships with her family and friends went along smoothly. Until the Professor came along, there had not been a single time that her parents had forbidden her to do anything she really wanted to do. And she had never been grounded! Mom and Dad had been so unfair!

But the Professor wasn't the one at fault any more than Eric. She was the one who had messed up, trying to go to the Professor's house against her parents wishes. She guessed that by the time Eric had told her that incredible tale of space travel through the Professor's telescope, she'd been so angry at herself and her parents that she had not really even been listening. Worse yet, she had accused him of lying!

The tears that quietly made their way down her face now were not for Eric alone. They were tears of shame. What an idiot I am, thought Meredith. Eric wouldn't lie! He's never lied to anyone, especially not to me. And that means – Oh, my gosh! She sat up straight in her chair. Eric somehow really *did* travel through space! She did not know how this could be possible but she did know now, without a doubt, that it *was* possible. Eric was telling the truth!

She jumped, startled as the bell rang, signaling the end of class. She waited impatiently as Mr. Kincaid explained their assignment for the following day. Without even writing it down, as was her usual custom, she crammed her things into her backpack and hurried across the classroom. She skidded to a stop in front of Eric's desk, practically knocking it over. He looked up, surprised.

"What's the big idea? "

"C'mon, Eric," said Meredith. She grabbed his backpack strap and a large portion of his shirtsleeve and began dragging him toward the door.

"Where are we going?" he asked. She did not answer, but pushed her way through several groups of students who were gathered here and there in the midst of after school conversations.

"What are you doing?" Eric pulled away from her and stopped in the middle of the hallway. "I'm not going another step until you tell me what's going on!"

She faced him and smiled, but Eric did not respond.

"I owe you an apology," she said. Her expression sobered. "I should have known you'd never lie to me. I was just jealous."

Eric stood frowning, silently considering her words. He was still for so long that Meredith began to fidget nervously.

"C'mon, Eric. Please forgive me?"

"Why should I?" he asked.

"Because when someone is really sorry, you're obligated to forgive them."

"Obligated, huh?"

" I'm not going another step ...."

"Yes, obligated. Compelled, duty-bound . . ." At his raised eyebrow she stopped her imitation of a thesaurus and continued on a somewhat safer path. "More to the point, I miss you. My life is considerably less interesting without you in it."

Finally Eric spoke. "Are you sure? I'm pretty gullible, you know."

"I can do gullible," she said.

"And some pretty wild things have been happening to me lately," he added.

"I can handle wild," she countered.

"And you'll believe me next time no matter how ridiculous or impossible I sound?" he asked.

"I stand ready to believe the ridiculous and impossible," she said, but while she echoed the seriousness in Eric's voice, a ripple of humor had begun to play around the corners of her mouth.

"And besides," she added. "You owe me a look through that telescope!" She smiled again; a big grin of challenge and invitation, and this time Eric grinned back.

Chapter 9

Meredith hurried home under gathering clouds heavy with rain. Only an hour before her heart had been as leaden as the sky, now her spirits soared. Everything was right again, and her happiness more than made up for the lack of sunshine.

She should never have doubted Eric for a moment. What a waste of time! They could have spent the entire week planning for their next visit to the observatory. As it was, they used their time after school discussing ways to convince the Professor to explain, well . . . everything! Now my special task, thought Meredith, is to convince Mom and Dad to lift my grounding restrictions a day early.

Eric had insisted that he call the Professor and put off their Friday night session until Saturday, in the hopes that by then she might have secured her release from 'prison'. Meredith was secretly pleased that Eric had offered to give up an evening of viewing on her behalf. She still felt horrible about the way she had acted though, so outwardly she encouraged him to go anyway and learn as much as he could in her absence. And this time, she had told him, make sure you remember names and places!

If Eric was surprised at her change of attitude, he hadn't shown it. He had seemed as relieved as she was to have things back to normal between them. She was glad that Eric was not in the habit of holding a grudge like some of her girlfriends. They could be a major pain sometimes.

Sandy met her at the door, wagging his big floppy tail. He followed her around as she hung up her coat and put her school things away, hoping as usual to get in on her afternoon snack. She tossed him a piece of cheese as she sat down at the kitchen table to start on her homework.

She worked at her math for a while. Normally she enjoyed completing her advanced algebra assignment; it was the only part of her homework she found challenging. Her teacher let her work through the text at her own pace so she wouldn't get bored. But tonight she was having trouble concentrating. Friday was approaching quickly and so far, her dad had not made time in his busy schedule to meet the Professor.

They were just finishing dinner that evening when her father handed her a sealed envelope.

"What's this, Dad?" she asked.

"These are the papers you asked me to sign." Meredith gasped and her eyes widened in surprise. She could hardly believe it! She looked at her mother for confirmation, and received a bright smile.

"I checked this guy out with all the references he gave," said her dad, "and I was still a little skeptical. But Mrs. Spencer called me at my office today and told me how much Eric enjoyed his session at the observatory last week and that he came home safe and sound. I decided this Professor of yours must be an okay guy, so I got off work early today and went over there."

He smiled, pleased at the look on his daughter's face.

"What was it like, Dad?"

"Dr. Strang has an incredible set up. I can hardly wait for you to see it. That telescope is the most amazing thing I've ever seen. Why, the advanced technology used in its construction is nothing short of genius."

Meredith couldn't contain herself any longer. "Oh, gee Dad! Thank you! Thank you so much!" She threw her arms around his neck, nearly knocking her dishes to the floor.

"You're welcome." He laughed, pretending to choke and cough as he untangled her arms. Then he became serious once more. "Actually, I got on quite well with Dr. Strang. He's an amazing person. Quite knowledgeable in a number of areas, including my own. There are not many people who can discuss nano-technology on more than a very basic level. "

"Does this mean I can go to the observatory, Dad?"

"Well . . .," he hesitated. "I told you the good news first."

Oh-oh, she thought. Aloud she said, "Okay, Dad. I think I already know the bad news, but hit me with it anyway."

"You're still grounded until Saturday."

Her face fell. She knew what that meant!

"Dear," her mother's voice broke in. "Couldn't we be a little lenient? After all, this is the first time -."

"No, I don't think so, Monica. You see, I believe there's more to this story than we were originally told."

Meredith cast an accusing stare across the table at her sister.

"I didn't say a word!" Katie jumped to her own defense.

"Settle down, both of you!" said Mr. Weatherford. "Katie wasn't the informant. You were ratted out by the neighbors. Keith Taylor saw you two and the dog walking along the roadside over by Mountain Lane last Friday night."

"Isn't that over by the bluff?" asked her mother. "Oh, Meredith! What were you thinking? Sandy could have been hurt, or worse! One of you could have fallen over the edge! Why were you clear over there?"

Meredith hung her head. "I was going to see if I could find the observatory. I'm really sorry Mom. I just wanted to see where it was. I was going to go up and knock on the door and say hi, and then I was going to come right home. Honest! But then Sandy started barking at something and ran off."

"And why didn't you tell us this the night Sandy ran away, dear?" asked Mrs. Weatherford.

"I – I was afraid if I did you would never let me go to Professor Strang's house," she said in a quiet voice. "And now that you know the truth, you never will." She stared miserably at the table.

"Well, before you get to feeling too sorry for yourself . . ." Her father picked up the envelope that he had given her earlier and tapped her nose lightly with the corner. She had completely forgotten about the permission form! She looked up quickly and was met by her father's broad smile. "I couldn't let you miss out on the chance of a lifetime because of a single mistake, honey," he explained.

"Oh, Dad! Can I really go?"

"Next week."

Meredith hugged him tightly. For the second time that day, she was crying, but these were tears of joy.

* * * * * * *

Eric thought that Friday would never arrive. The day had dawned foggy because of yesterday's rain, but Meredith had been confident that the fog would burn off before noon. As usual she was right, and tonight's viewing was bound to be spectacular.

Meredith had met him at school breathless and excited that morning.

"He signed it!" Her braids bounced as she jumped up and down. At that moment, Eric thought she looked a lot like her little sister. He did not need to ask what she was referring to. "Really?" he asked. "That's great! What made him change his mind?"

"Not a what but a who, actually. Your mother. She called Dad and explained to him that the Professor hadn't hacked you up and buried you in his backyard or anything. He actually took off work and spent the entire afternoon over there, if you can believe that! I think he and Professor Strang really liked each other. Anyway, will you tell your mom 'thanks' for me? She's fantastic!"

"Yeah, she is pretty cool sometimes." Eric mentally wrote himself a reminder to give his mom three giant hugs tonight and never forget to take out the garbage again. He owed her that much, at least!

"So you can come with me?" he asked.

"No," Meredith said sadly as they parted to attend their first class. "I *am* still grounded, but I can go with you next week. Gosh, I hope I don't miss anything."

Eric thought it was highly likely that Meredith would miss out on a whole lot, but he did not voice his opinion out loud. Things had just gotten back to normal, and he certainly didn't want a repeat of last week.

During every spare moment of that day Meredith wrote questions to ask the Professor on Eric's notebooks and book covers. Questions like 'What's the magnitude limit?' and 'Does the scope work from an integrated, computerized star chart database?' were crowded into the margins of his math and science assignments. She was driving him crazy!

"You know, I'm not planning to take all these books and things over to Professor Strang's house tonight. I can't remember all this stuff. Why don't we just wait 'til next week and then you can do the asking? Besides," he added, "I'm not going to understand half the answers."

"You don't understand half the questions!" she said playfully, pushing him from behind. "Now get going. You're never going to get there if you don't go home and eat dinner."

"Yes mother," he said sarcastically. She made a face and pushed him again in the direction of home.

Eric hurried through his chores and by twilight was in a fever of anticipation. He had worn a path in the carpet between the kitchen table and the front window watching for his mom to pull into the driveway, and another to the windows in the back of the house checking on the weather. The forecast had been for scattered showers sometime before Saturday morning, but so far the skies looked clear.

If his mother noticed his impatience during dinner she said nothing about it, other than telling him to chew his food rather than inhale it. If anyone had asked him what he'd eaten, he could not have told them. He sat across the table watching her eat trying not to tap his fingers or swing his feet. He was not totally successful. Finally, he resigned himself to the fact that his mother was not willing to be hurried through her meal.

"How are things going at school?" she asked.

"Pretty good, I guess. I turned in my history project on time and everything," he answered.

"I mean how are things working out with you and Meredith?"

"Good. We talked today and everything's fine."

"She's not upset with you anymore?"

Eric grabbed a piece of bread and stuffed some in his mouth without buttering it. "Hmm umm." He shook his head.

"Is she coming along tonight?" Finishing the last bite of food, Eric's mom began to clear the table.

"I don't think so," he mumbled around the bread. The look his mother gave him was more effective than words. He chewed and swallowed before he added, "she had something else to do tonight." Eric knew his mom was on a fishing expedition to find out if the Weatherfords had taken her advice about the Professor, so he got up and circled the table to where she was stacking dishes. He gave her a tremendous hug, plates and all.

"What's that for?" she asked.

"That's from Meredith," he said. "She told me you called her dad. He met the Professor, so she'll be able to go next week. And this," he hugged her again, "is from me. Thanks, Mom."

"You're very welcome." She was glad that the two friends had worked things out.

"All right, Mr. Wizard. Grab your coat and let's go," she said. "Science waits for no man."

"Who's Mr. Wizard?" he asked.

"Mr. Wizard was a guy on TV years ago that used to do scientific experiments and then explain them."

"Oh." Eric thought that the title of Mr. Wizard did not fit him at all. He did not consider himself a science whiz by any means. His grades in biology last quarter were proof of that! However, the name seemed to fit his new mentor perfectly. He wondered if Professor Strang knew about Mr. Wizard.

The drive to Mountain Lane took only a few minutes. As Eric leapt out of the car, he heard his mom call to him.

"Pick you up at 11:00."

"'Kay, Mom. Thanks!" He dashed up the front walk and as he knocked, he was surprised to see lights on inside the house. He questioned the Professor about this as he was welcomed and ushered through the living room. Now that he could see his surroundings, Eric thought the room was much less eerie than it had seemed the week before. In fact, it was an extremely ordinary room, which held little evidence of the personality of the man who lived in it.

"I thought after last week your mother might feel a little uncomfortable dropping you off at a dark house. Besides, I had a few things to put in order in the observatory before we start tonight's session. Will Miss Weatherford be joining us this evening?"

"No, sir. She's ground-. I mean, there was something else she had to do." Eric knew that Meredith would not want him broadcasting her predicament; especially not to someone she had hardly met.

"I see." The Professor smiled and for the first time, Eric had a chance to closely study his face. His brown eyes were merry and surrounded by laugh lines and he held the boy's attention with his direct and honest gaze. His hair was brown, too, except in a few places where some gray was starting to show. Eric wondered how old the Professor was, and was on the verge of asking when without any warning, the lights went out.

This sudden darkness caught him off guard. During their previous session, Eric had gotten used to having the lights respond to a quietly spoken word or two, but this time he had heard nothing.

"These lights aren't operated by the computer?" asked Eric in surprise.

"No. Simple switches here."

This time Eric heard a slight clicking sound as the lights went on and off again. "Thanks for the demonstration," he said.

The Professor ignored the sarcasm in the boy's voice. "You're quite welcome," he said. "Shall we go upstairs?"

"Sure. Can we look at Saturn again? That was really neat."

"Patience, my young friend. Perhaps you might like to amuse yourself while we wait for full darkness by looking through my collection. Go on, help yourself."

There was much more to the observatory than Eric had been able to see on his first visit. This evening, with the dome closed the room was warmer and its white expanse reflected the bright light back into the room. One entire side of the circular space was devoted to a long worktable that cleverly conformed to the curvature of the wall it was attached to. The shelves above the work area were filled with hundreds of books of various sizes and shapes. There were portfolios as well, with enlarged photographs carefully pressed between their covers, probably some of the same pictures the Professor had used in the classroom that day.

The table itself was covered with every kind of long distance viewing device that Eric had ever heard of, and a few that he hadn't, from the smallest set of binoculars to something that looked like it might be a telescope but appeared to be made out of a box. Several of these items seemed to be in various stages of assembly and disassembly. Interspersed amongst them were also a microscope, a View-Master toy, and several pairs of reading glasses.

Turning toward the light, Eric picked up the toy and held it to his eyes. What he saw through the View-Master startled him, for it was a brilliant spiral suspended in velvety blackness. The image looked exactly like the galaxy that he had gotten an uncomfortably close glimpse of through the telescope last week. He looked for the picture's caption which appeared in the rectangular space between the lenses. It read: 'The Andromeda Galaxy – 2.26 million light years from Earth.' That was the name I couldn't remember, he thought.

Pleased that he had discovered that little tidbit of information without anyone's help, Eric carefully placed the child's toy back where he had found it. He wondered if the Professor had used just such a picture to trick him into thinking that he had been transported light years across space. Was it possible to project an image like this one into the eyepiece of a telescope? Perhaps there *was* a simple explanation for what he had seen, but it would take someone a lot smarter than him to figure it out. Someone like Meredith.

"What's this, Professor?" He pointed to one of the strange combinations of photographs and lenses that he had not been able to identify.

"That is one of my prize possessions; a stereoscopic viewer." The Professor crossed the room with long strides and picked up the object carefully holding it out to the boy. "It was invented in 1838 by Sir Charles Wheatstone. Would you like to try it?"

"What does it do?" With exaggerated care, Eric lifted the heavy viewer. "Wait! I know. It makes a 3-D picture."

"Quite right, Eric. Like the toy you were just holding, it combines two slightly different images into one, creating a 3 dimensional image. Leonardo da Vinci was one of the first scientists to experiment with this technology, back in the 15th century. "

"I thought da Vinci was an artist. Didn't he paint the Mona Lisa?"

"Yes, he did." The Professor sounded surprised. "But he was also a doctor, a sculptor, an aeronautical engineer, a scientist, and an astronomer."

"Wow! He was a whole lot of people!"

"Exactly why he was considered to be a Renaissance man; a master of any trade he put his hand to. The Renaissance was the beginning of an entirely new age in history, a time when man replaced ignorance with knowledge and pessimism with hope."

Eric tried to pay close attention to everything the Professor said, but the conversation had begun to wander into that foggy, gray area between being interesting and being way over his head.

"I apologize, Eric. I sometimes forget that I'm no longer at the University." The Professor laughed. "I miss telling everything I know to a captive audience."

Eric carefully set the antique viewer back on the table, and noticed a small, silver object just inches from his hand. Curious, he picked it up, turning it over and over. It looked like a cross between a calculator and an electronic game. Carefully flipping aside clear protective covers that opened like the wings of a small bird, he experimentally pressed several of the buttons located under what appeared to be a display screen.

"Kindly put me down," said a voice. "I am not a toy!"

With a surprised squeak, Eric dropped the object and then, afraid that he might have broken it, quickly picked it up again.

"P-P-Professor!" he stammered. "It talked!" He held the object stiffly at arms length, but the Professor made no move to take it from him, so Eric put it back on the worktable where he had found it.

"Allow me to introduce SID, whose initials stand for Scientific Interactive Database," said the Professor. "SID, Eric is our new student."

"Professor, please inform *your* new student that I am not a plaything," said the voice. "And I dislike being referred to as 'it'."

"Eric can hear you, SID. You may speak to him directly."

"If I choose to speak to him at all," answered the voice.

"Now, SID. Don't be difficult. I would like you and Eric to be friends."

Eric had been standing there silently, too stunned to move. Finally he blurted out, "What is it – he?"

"SID is a product of many years of private research. Into his database I have placed the sum total of all my knowledge and that of countless other scientists– astronomical, geological, mathematical. He is an integral

" Kindly put me down. I am not a toy! "

part of the operation of this observatory. He is my colleague, my research assistant, and my friend."

"Pleased to meet you," said Eric hesitantly.

"Oh, the pleasure is all mine," said SID. Eric thought that the voice sounded far from pleased. In fact, it, or he, sounded downright disagreeable. None of the computers in Eric's experience had ever spoken to him that way but then, they had not spoken to him at all!

"Come along, Eric. SID will assist us with our viewing this evening." The Professor retrieved the device from the worktable and ascended the ladder to the telescope viewing station. Eric watched, fascinated, as SID was attached to the base of the telescope within a rectangular alcove just large enough for his streamlined form. A green light blinked regularly on his display screen.

"This is an ACT Receptacle," the Professor explained, "from which SID performs many of his functions."

"What exactly are *his* functions?" Eric gave his words special emphasis. He did not want to risk hurting SID's feelings again. Shaking his head, he thought, a game with feelings? What next? He followed the Professor up the ladder and stood beside him on the platform.

Professor Strang seemed to consider Eric's question carefully. "As I stated earlier, SID does indeed serve as my assistant. Among other things, he performs spectral analyses, keeps accurate records of recent advances in stellar cartography, and performs periodic maintenance checks on the Discovery VII and its computer."

Meredith, where are you when I need you, thought Eric. There was a word or two in there I recognized, but the rest went completely over my head. I think I'm going to need a taller ladder!

SID's green light continued to flash on and off, but nothing seemed to be happening. Eric moved in for a closer inspection to see if he could determine where the thing's voice was coming from, at least.

"What are you looking at, little boy?" asked SID.

Startled, Eric jerked away violently, knocking to the floor several of the little spheres from the Professor's demonstration the previous week. They spun away into the darkness and disappeared.

"So much for the planet Earth," muttered the Professor dryly.

"Sorry," said Eric. "But I'm not a little boy. I'm in the eighth grade!"

"I rest my case!" said SID.

"Mind your manners, SID," cautioned the Professor. "Would you open the dome please, and rotate to 214 degrees? Eric would like to look at Saturn. Oh, and SID, get the lights, will you?"

"Yes, Professor." SID's sigh was so loud that it could have been heard from across the observatory. Then, in a stage whisper that was meant to be heard also, he added, "but we looked at Saturn last week."

Eric was still examining the database closely, so that the sudden movement of the platform caught him completely off guard. He lost his footing and felt the side of his face come into painful contact with the metal railing.

"Are you all right?" asked the Professor with concern, "Do you need some ice?"

"No. It's just a bump," Eric responded, rubbing his cheek. "Graceful, huh?"

After a second look to confirm that Eric was not seriously hurt, the Professor waved his young student to the eyepiece.

Suddenly, Eric was reluctant to step into position. His mind had been so distracted by meeting SID he'd completely forgotten his intention to confront the Professor directly about last week's adventure. Now that he was faced with the prospect of repeating that escapade, his questions became like jelly, seeping through the cracks of his overtaxed brain. He didn't want to ask anything anyway in the presence of his mentor's super-critical silver companion.

"Is something the matter?" asked the Professor.

Before Eric could answer, SID spoke up, again whispering. "Yes. The boy is suffering from brain freeze."

"ENOUGH!" The Professor's threatening hand hovered over SID's receptacle.

"All right! I promise I'll behave, Professor. Besides, if you disconnect me, our scheduled research for this evening will remain incomplete." SID's voice had the same wheedling tone that Eric occasionally used when he wanted a favor from his mother that she was unwilling to grant.

Scheduled research? That sounded interesting, if he could get past this SID's towering attitude problem.

"Here we go, Eric." said the Professor. "Step up. The telescope is all set." Again he found himself ushered toward the eyepiece. There was Saturn, just as he had seen it the last time.

"Fantastic!" said Eric.

"Why don't we give our young friend a closer view?" suggested the Professor.

"If you insist," answered SID.

Sucked down into a sliding, whirling vortex, Eric had no chance to object before the blackness of deepest space enveloped him.

Chapter 10

Someone was screaming. As soon as Eric figured out who it was, he stopped. What he saw when he opened his eyes nearly made him begin again. He was suspended in space above the ringed planet.

He panicked! It's happened again! Up until this moment, even amidst his protest to the contrary, he'd half suspected that Meredith was right, that he *had* fallen asleep and dreamed his journey to Andromeda. But now he was experiencing the same sensations as before and could not deny that he was millions of miles from home. He found with little humor that a line from the Wizard of Oz kept repeating itself over and over in his head. 'Toto, I've got a feeling we're not in Kansas anymore.' Well I've got news for you, Dorothy, thought Eric. I've got a feeling we're not on the planet Earth anymore!

As his breathing slowed, the dizziness that had made his head spin subsided and he was able to think more clearly. The sensation that he was falling disappeared, as well, and he was left with only a dull, throbbing ache over his eyes. He didn't seem to be in any immediate danger. He was lying face down on a surface that was as solid as any regular floor, but was completely transparent. Spread out beneath him were the luminous hues of Saturn's rings, more a subdued shade of purple now than the oranges and yellows he had seen from the observatory. The planet's sphere, although only partially visible, loomed over its rings, filling his entire vista with a monstrous presence.

Carefully, he stood up on quivering legs. He put his hands out in front of him and met a smooth surface that felt like glass, but when he rapped on it with his knuckles, there was no sound. The barrier shimmered at his touch however, and Eric could just see the glimmering edges of the wall that encased him. He experimented further by reaching above his head and from side to side. At each contact there was a slight flicker that left his fingertips tingling, almost as if he had touched an exposed electrical source.

I'm in a giant bubble, he thought. A space ship! How is this possible? Where did it come from? He heard a quiet beeping sound and turned to discover its source. Lights of many colors blinked on and off at irregular intervals. Eric supposed that each of these lights was an indicator of one of the ship's functions, but after watching the flashing array for several minutes he could figure out none of its meaning. He seated himself on a high stool that was fastened to the floor facing the console. He was careful of moving more than a few inches in either direction in the confined space for fear that he would touch something that would interfere with the workings of the ship.

Okay, he thought. Let's get a grip on reality here. I was in the Professor's observatory talking to him and that SID thing. I looked in the telescope and now, I'm here. In outer space. In some sort of bubble. He began to inventory his situation. The air in here smells kind of funny. I'm not bouncing off the walls, so this ship must have some way of making its own gravity. And heat, too. It's a little cold in here, but not bad considering its freezing out there. I guess I've got everything I need.

"So why am I here?" Eric wondered aloud.

"I asked myself that same question, only moments ago." Eric was so surprised by the familiar voice that he fell off the stool.

"SID? Is that you?" From his place on the floor, Eric examined each surface intently until he located SID inside his now familiar receptacle on the computer console just to the left of a group of flashing yellow lights.

"How did you get here? You were back at the observatory."

"So were you," said the computer.

"Oh. Right." Not really an answer thought Eric, but considering this is SID, maybe that's the best I'm gonna get. He decided to try a different tack.

"What are you doing here?"

"I am attempting to perform an atmospheric density scan."

"An atmosphere dense what?" asked Eric, confused. "No, I mean what are you – what are *we* doing here, out in space in this bubble thingy?" He got up from the floor and reseated himself on the stool.

"My, my. You have an amazing command of the English language," said SID with a sneer. "This 'bubble thingy', as you call it, is a cosmosphere."

"A cosmosphere?"

"Yes. It is a self contained environmental unit that is capable of transporting the operator anywhere in the universe that is accessible to the Discovery VII Telescope. The Professor calls it the Chrysalis."

"Okay, so what are we doing here?" Eric repeated his earlier question. "What am *I* supposed to do? Why didn't the Professor warn me before -."

"Young man," SID interrupted, "you must limit yourself to one question at a time. *I* am here to perform research. *You* are here to observe. And as to why Professor Strang did not warn you of the telescope's capabilities prior to initiating this voyage, I do not know. I imagine he wanted to measure your reaction to the unknown which, as far as I can see, is the response one would expect of any underdeveloped, undisciplined child such as yourself."

Eric wasn't sure if what SID had just said was meant to be an insult but just in case, he ignored it.

"But I'm not qualified for this. Why would he send me?" Eric asked thoughtfully.

"That question can be answered only by the Professor himself. I am completely at a loss as to why he chose you for this momentous experiment or to be his apprentice for that matter. After all, you are only a student; your interest in the sciences is totally lacking, you have absolutely no background in research, and you are entirely too young!" SID finished with a flourish.

"Okay, Okay! Stop trying to cheer me up! I get your point. But you're stuck with me for the time being, so we might as well make the best of it. You never know. I might come in handy." Eric couldn't imagine any way in which he could possibly be useful, but he was getting a little fed up with being put down by this conceited computer.

Eric sat in silence for a few moments, content to watch Saturn turn beneath him. He still could not get over the wonder of it. Here he was; ordinary Eric Spencer, in space! The feeling of awe was soon broken though, by an audible rumbling in his stomach.

"Is there anything to eat?" asked Eric tentatively. "I'm kinda hungry."

"I'm a computer, not a flight attendant," said SID. "You'll just have to wait until our return."

"And when will that be?"

"We shall be called back to the observatory in precisely 27.35 minutes. If you will open that small compartment to your left, you will find water there. Hopefully that will be sufficient."

Eric did as he was told and found several liters of bottled water.

"Wow, they're even cold."

"All the comforts of home." SID now sounded quite pleased with himself.

"You guys should think of putting in a vending machine. You know, Galaxy Chips, Black Hole Blasters, Globular Clusters. I really like the purple-flavored ones. Might be a big seller out here. I could use a couple of aspirin, too. I've got a headache the size of that planet out there," said Eric.

"Sorry, no aspirin. The pain you're experiencing is the unfortunate result of the transference. We're still working out the bugs."

"You send me millions of miles out in space and now you tell me you've got bugs?" Eric asked incredulously.

"*I* do not have bugs. The procedure does. Traveling at the speed of thought is a totally new and innovative method of moving from one place to another. It involves tapping into the human mind and when one does that, one never knows what the end result will be."

"What's that supposed to mean?"

"It means that you should be happy that all you've ended up with is a little headache. Besides, there's no need for concern. The Professor's made hundreds of jumps and his neural pathways have never been scrambled. Not that I know of, anyway!"

"Gee, I feel so much better now," said Eric sarcastically.

"You humans! You worry too much. Are you ready to get some work done, or are you going to continue being difficult?"

"As difficult as a talking T. V. remote?"

"Very funny," said SID. "If you are finished amusing yourself, you could occupy the remaining time by assisting me with these experiments. It is a rather long list for the short amount of time we were given, however Professor Strang has the utmost confidence in my ability to complete them. Now, pay attention."

SID proceeded to show him the digital readouts for life support and environmental controls. He patiently explained the purpose of each flashing light and briefly demonstrated the craft's manual control systems.

"Do you mean that I could fly this ship with these controls here?" Eric asked.

"An experienced pilot could fly this craft using manual controls," corrected SID snippily. "You on the other hand . . ."

"How does it work? I mean, where are the engines?" Eric remembered SID's charge earlier to ask only one thing at a time and hoped his double question would go unnoticed. SID did not seem to mind this time. In fact, he appeared to be enjoying his new role as Eric's instructor.

"Once a person has arrived at the transference point set by the telescope, the Chrysalis operates like any normal space craft," he explained. "With the exception that the ship's propulsion system is nothing so clumsy as rocket fuel or nuclear power."

"What kind of power does it use?"

"Ion propulsion," SID pronounced proudly.

"Ions! That's science fiction!"

"Science fact," corrected the computer. "Ion power is the most efficient in the universe; a chemically inert gas, environmentally harmless, that yields 3.4 horsepower when exposed to the light of the sun. Zero to sixty in about 40 hours."

"Hmm," said Eric, unimpressed. "Fast."

"It won't win any races, I'll admit, but given enough time, it will get you where you want to go! Now enough questions. Do you want to be my assistant or not?"

Eric was amazed at how easy it was to think of SID as a real person. He had to continually remind himself that this was a computer he was talking to. He still wasn't sure he was willing to be told what to do by a machine, especially one with an attitude like SID's, but at this point he couldn't think of a better plan. Besides, he rather liked the idea of SID having to ask for his help.

"What do I do?" he asked.

"Do you see the pattern of yellow lights on the display panel to your left?"

"Yes," answered Eric.

"Press the touch screen above the middle one."

Eric did as he was directed, and heard a swishing sound like air moving through a hollow tube. He pulled his hand back, startled. "What happened?" he asked.

"You launched a Class 4 atmospheric probe."

"I did? What will that do?"

"The probe will gather readings of Saturn's atmospheric pressure, temperature, and composition, and then it will send its findings to the main database of the Chrysalis," explained the computer.

"How come we're doing all these tests? Haven't there been a bunch of probes sent out here before to find out all this stuff?"

"Press the touch screen above the middle one."

"There have been three spacecrafts that have flown past Saturn. NASA launched two Voyager missions in 1977, one of which did a flyby in November 1981 and the other which reached Saturn in August of the same year. The planet and some of its moons were photographed extensively. However, the closest approach was 62,600 miles; we are much closer than that, now."

"Why were there two missions?"

"Different destinations. Both crafts were designed to take advantage of Saturn's considerable gravity as a slingshot. Voyager II continued on to Uranus in 1986 and Neptune in 1989, while Voyager I sailed past the outer planets and in 1998 became the most distant man made object in the universe."

"How do they know that?"

"NASA scientists are still in contact with both Voyager I and II, and are confident that they will maintain contact until approximately the year 2020."

"Wow! That's cool!" Eric was surprised to find he was enjoying SID's miniature lecture on the history of space exploration. "Didn't you say there were three missions to Saturn?"

"Yes. The third was the Cassini-Huygens mission launched in October of 1997; named for Giovanni Cassini, a 17th century astronomer who, with the aid of the telescopes of his day, was the first to discover that a gap existed between the rings. It reached Saturn in July of 2004. In January of the following year, the Huygens probe landed on Titan, Saturn's largest moon. Many of its instruments are earlier versions of those carried aboard the Chrysalis. They measure mass, magnetic fields, particle density and a host of other things. Since we are currently nearer to Saturn than any NASA probe has ever been, we will be conducting tests that have never been done. This is an exhilarating moment for the Professor. "

"And for you, too, I bet."

"Please. I don't allow myself to become excited."

"Yeah, right. So, then, the Professor's going to become famous."

"Famous? Hardly," said SID regretfully.

"What do you mean? All this new research, the telescope, and everything? Surely scientists are gonna be crazy to hear about all of it!"

"They will never hear about it." At the boy's shocked expression, SID explained. "The Discovery VII is an invention whose secret must never be revealed."

"But why?"

"That is something that Professor Strang must explain to you." SID overrode Eric's sputtering protests and returned to his former businesslike manner.

"Now," said SID, "while I bring the Chrysalis into position above the Cassini division, will you extend the telescoping probe arm to twenty meters? It is already equipped with a solar gel collector."

Eric knew the little computer was just testing him; SID could have performed any of these functions on his own. Anxious to prove himself, Eric looked hopelessly across the panel, wishing the right screen would somehow reveal itself. Remarkably it did, for there in front of him under the view screen were a collection of controls, one of which read 'Probe Extension'. Impulsively and without asking, he pushed it and a metered gauge appeared before him on the screen.

"Not bad," said SID.

Eric's confidence soared. He put his finger on the gauge and drew it out to the requested distance, giving SID a look that said, 'So, there! Not as dumb as you thought, am I?'

Watching through the clear bubble, Eric saw a long thin arm reaching out from the Chrysalis toward the planet's rings. At its end was a device that looked like a common tennis racket, with a light green waffle where its strings should have been.

"What's that?" asked Eric.

"That is a particulate gel sampling matrix, designed to collect minute dust and fine particles from space. Astronomers believe that Saturn's rings are made mainly of ice, sand, and dust; the same materials that went into the composition of many of the planets - including Earth. The matrix will gather particles which will be stored and analyzed in Professor Strang's laboratory later."

"The Professor has a laboratory, too? Excellent!" said Eric.

"Brilliant, actually," said SID. "Everything the Professor has invented has been pure genius. Present company included."

"Don't you think that sounds a little conceited? I mean, you're just a computer."

"I am much more than a mere computer, young man. I am a Series 2000 Scientific Interactive Database with enhanced biotronic memory engrams. I have an unlimited capacity for processing information and you don't -"

"All right, all right! Don't get your nanites in a knot! I didn't mean to hurt your feelings." By now it was evident to Eric that SID did indeed have feelings, and that they were easily bruised. He agreed that Professor Strang was a brilliant scientist to have created all this; the observatory, the telescope, the Chrysalis, but he wondered if it had been such a great idea to invent a computer that had the emotional stability of a seven year old to run it all!

The monitor screen lit up and began to display a series of numbers. Eric supposed it was the data from the probe, but he had no idea what to do next.

"Um, SID? " He tapped gently on the console. "There's, like, a bunch of numbers and stuff. Should I, um, do anything with them?"

The computer was silent.

"C'mon, SID. I really am sorry," said Eric. "C'mon, answer me, will ya? Give me a break. I didn't even know that a computer could have feelings until today."

Finally SID spoke.

"The main computer will automatically record the data from the probe." Then he sighed. "Human emotions are such a trial, Eric. It's not enough that I'm expected to perform experiments and collect data. I must deal with feelings as well. Messy, inconsistent things! I don't know what the Professor was thinking."

Eric was surprised that the computer would talk so openly with him. He'd even called him by name. I thought he didn't like me, he said to himself. Maybe he just needs somebody to talk to, somebody to be his friend. It's worth a try, anyway.

"Why did Professor Strang give you feelings? Isn't that kinda – different, for a computer?" asked Eric.

"Everything the Professor does is 'different'. He's a brilliant man, I tell you. He wanted me to be able to interact with humans on their level; to learn and adapt in the same way a human being does. He developed a method of programming a living human's personality traits onto the main memory circuits of a computer. That way the essence of that person's humanity can be maintained indefinitely. That is how I came into being."

Eric wasn't quite sure he understood. "Do you mean that the Professor can keep a person's thoughts, a person's feelings, alive inside a computer? "

"Essentially, that is correct," answered SID.

"And that's how he made you? Who did he–"

"The Professor has informed me that our time is up." SID said abruptly. He seemed anxious to change the subject.

"The Professor! Can you talk to him from here?"

"Of course. I have been in contact with Professor Strang from the moment we left the observatory. He suggests that you strap yourself into the safety seat. As you have recently discovered, the effects of thought transference can be rather unsettling to you humans. Fortunately, I am immune to such disturbances."

Thought transference? That's the second time tonight SID has mentioned something about that. Wonder what that's all about? He stored the question away for later. Then he noticed that a high-backed, deeply padded chair had appeared as if by magic at the end of the console. Eric quickly harnessed himself in.

"Can Professor Strange hear me?" he asked.

"Negative. However I could relay a message for you, if you wish."

Eric thought about that for a moment. The computer and he had come to somewhat of an understanding during the last hour, yet he wasn't sure if he trusted SID to convey a message without adding more of his own caustic remarks.

"No, thank you," said Eric. But I'll have plenty of things to say to him later, he thought.

Chapter 11

"We're back!" Eric's triumphant shout sounded almost simultaneously with SID's more reserved statement of fact that they had indeed returned. The computer's voice however, held no less enthusiasm than that of the boy.

Professor Strang met Eric at the bottom of the ladder with a wide smile and a hearty handshake.

"Well done my boy, well done," he said.

"A-hem." SID cleared his throat noisily from his ACT Receptacle. "And am I not to be congratulated also? I was, after all, completely responsible for this mission and its success. The boy here, was merely along for the ride."

"Of course you are to be congratulated, SID. You performed your required functions perfectly, as usual. I couldn't be more pleased. The results of your research have been pouring in for the past half hour. However, don't count yourself the only factor in the successful completion of tonight's journey. Eric was an important part of our experiment."

"Really? Well, if you say so, Professor." SID was not convinced. "If you'll excuse me I will analyze and catalogue the data we have just received, seeing as how I am no longer needed here."

"As you like, SID." The Professor turned his attention back to Eric. Noticing the concerned frown on the boy's face, he continued. "Don't worry about SID, Eric. He has some unresolved issues. Or is that frown for me? I admit it was inexcusable of me to trick you into an unexpected space voyage that way. I hope you will allow me to apologize."

"Apologize? Are you serious? That was the most fantastic thing that's ever happened to me in my whole life! Besides, now I know for sure I'm not crazy!"

"What do you mean? Of course you're not crazy!"

"*I* thought I was. And so did Meredith. You see Professor, last week when I was here I kinda, well . . ."

"Go on, I'm listening."

"Well, I pressed some button on the telescope by mistake and I ended up going to the . . . darn it, I can never remember that name."

"The Andromeda Galaxy?"

"That's it! The Andromeda Galaxy. I was only there for a couple of seconds. But I was afraid to say anything about it. I was afraid you'd think I was unstable or something, and then you wouldn't let – hey! Stop laughing! It's not funny."

"I'm sorry," said the Professor, still chuckling. "But you should have seen your face!"

"You knew all the time!" accused Eric.

"Of course I knew. You came back white as a ghost. The only thing that kept you from collapsing in a heap was pure stubbornness! In that capacity, you bear a strong resemblance to our little digital friend here."

"If I were truly listening, I would be insulted," interjected the computer. The Professor ignored him. So did Eric; he was learning.

"Besides," the Professor continued, "SID told me. He actually thought your mistake was a fortunate event. A sort of pretest to determine if you would be able to use the telescope at all. It was just a quick trip. He didn't think you could do it, but I had every confidence in you, boy."

"Gee, thanks. Wish I felt that way. I couldn't even get Meredith to believe me, at least at first," Eric explained. "I tried to tell her all about it and, well, you can imagine how that conversation went."

"Meredith is a scientist. She finds it difficult to believe in anything that is not entirely logical. You, on the other hand are a dreamer; one who can grasp all the possibilities of the unimaginable."

"And you, Professor? What are you?"

"Haven't you guessed that by now, boy? Come, and I'll show you!" The Professor led him to the base of the Discovery VII Telescope.

"Many years ago, when I was considerably younger than I am now, I dreamed of traveling to the stars. My imagination was fed by some of the greatest writers of this century; Clarke, Heinlein, Asimov, to name just a few. Within the pages of their books I felt the first stirrings of an idea; an idea so improbable that I dared not even whisper it." As the Professor talked, he slowly circled the giant telescope. "Have you ever seen 'The Day the Earth Stood Still?'."

Eric shook his head. "What's that?"

"It's an old movie. Black and white."

"They had movies back then?" Eric joked.

The Professor laughed his big hearty laugh. "Of course they did. People actually talked in them, too."

Eric pretended to be surprised.

"My point is that these old movies were based on the premise that our galaxy is filled with other life forms, many of them intelligent," said the Professor. "These life forms have the capability of traversing the vast distances of space and time."

"Yeah, but didn't most of those aliens show up and like, trash the earth?" asked Eric.

"In many cases, yes. However, this particular story was about beings who valued life above all else; beings whose only interest in Earth was to prevent the unfortunate creatures living upon it from blowing themselves and their galactic neighbors to Kingdom Come."

"So, you think there is life out there?" asked Eric.

"Personally, yes. I believe that we humans would be terribly conceited to think that we are the only creatures important enough to crawl around on the surface of a planet for a few million years. However, the question of life on other planets is best left to philosophers and theologians. It is not the main thing that concerns me. Of course," Professor Strang chuckled, "if an alien life form were to amble in some day and request a nice hot cup of tea, I certainly would sit up and take notice."

The Professor stopped his slow circuit of the telescope and reached up, placing his hand lovingly on its brass body. "But, Eric, my main purpose was to discover whether it would actually be possible for a species such as ourselves to cross the colossal emptiness of space. That accomplishment would be an incredible feat!"

"Come on, Professor, did you really buy into all that space travel stuff? That was just science fiction," said Eric.

"Not all of it. Please tell me you've heard of NASA; the National Aeronautics and Space Administration?"

"Of course I have."

"Well, they put a man on the moon in 1969."

"Yeah, but that's a long way from the kind of space trip I just took!"

"So it is. But somebody had to imagine it could happen before it could be made to happen. There were many people who believed that space travel was just a figment of the imagination, even years after the Russian cosmonaut, Yuri Gagarin, proved that it was possible. Think where we would be if the great dreamers of our age had allowed themselves to be influenced, or worse yet interfered with by such narrow minded people."

"Where would we be?" asked Eric, shrugging his shoulders. "Pretty much where we are now, I guess. I mean, our lives don't actually depend on space travel."

"On the contrary, many of the products that enrich our lives and in some cases even save lives were developed from technology that was first employed by NASA and the space program. Take, for example, the heat proof shielding used in today's fire fighting equipment. That came about as a direct result of the space program's need to build a craft that could withstand the temperatures created when re-entering the earth's atmosphere."

"Is that why you made the telescope, Professor? To find new technology?"

"No, Eric, although that certainly would be a fine bi-product of my research. My reason for inventing this telescope is evident in its very name; the Discovery VII – created to discover and reveal the secrets of the universe to those who truly have the desire and the courage to unveil them."

Eric looked up at his mentor, sighing heavily. He had so many more questions he didn't know where to begin, but he offered up the one foremost on his mind.

"How does it work?"

"It's fairly complex," warned the Professor.

"I figured it would be," said Eric. "Just run the basics by me, okay?"

"All right. Remember the clock drive?"

"Yes. You told me about it that first night. It keeps the telescope looking at what you want it to, right?"

"Exactly. Well, the clock drive on the Discovery VII is connected to a unique system. When you touched the actuator," the Professor pointed to a touch pad just below SID's alcove, "it begins the process of translocation."

"That must be what I did last week," exclaimed Eric.

"Precisely," said the Professor. "At that moment, SID reached into your mind and converted your brain waves into digital energy. This energy was then 'piggybacked' to a concentrated beam of tachyon particles and sent to whatever location was programmed into the clock drive, in your case, Andromeda. I call it traveling at the speed of thought. Unfortunately, the effects of such travel can be somewhat disorienting."

"If you're talking about those headaches, I agree," said Eric.

The Professor grimaced.

"Yes. I'm sorry about that. It does get better though. As your confidence increases, and as you become more accustomed to having SID inside your mind, the headaches will go away."

"Where does the Chrysalis come in?"

"That's a bit harder to explain. It has to do with changing matter into energy; a similar process to the one I mentioned before. Let me just say that a very special relationship exists between the telescope, the space craft and our good friend SID."

"Where's the Chrysalis now?"

"The ship is stored here when not in use."

"Here?" Eric looked around quickly, expecting to see a spacecraft lurking in the shadows of the observatory.

"'Here' meaning digitally stored inside the telescope," explained the Professor. He touched the large ring that surrounded the base of the eyepiece. "This is the capacitance ring, where all of the digital information, mental and material alike, is stored before being sent on to its destination. The Chrysalis is always in the ring as a safeguard against sending someone out into space unprotected."

"Cool!" Eric stared at the Professor with a new appreciation of the man's genius.

"And now, Eric, if you'll excuse me for a few moments, I am very excited to see the results of the experiments that you helped SID perform." Professor Strang retrieved SID from his receptacle on the telescope's base.

"That's okay, Professor. If it's all right with you, I'll just sit here and try to get rid of this monster headache."

"Complaining again?" SID's voice broke into their conversation. "This boy's internal mechanism is permanently set at 'Whine'."

Eric remained silent. He was getting better and better at ignoring the computer's jabs. The Professor was already an expert at it. Eric could tell he'd had plenty of practice.

"By the way, Professor," continued the computer.

"What is it, SID?"

"I have not been successful in downloading all the data gathered by the Class 4 probe. I would be grateful for your assistance."

"You'll be fine here, Eric?"

"Sure."

The Professor cradled his small companion in his hand as he descended the ladder, entering data on the device's touch screen and muttering to himself. When he reached the workstation he set SID on the desk and turned his attention to the main computer. He appeared to have forgotten the boy completely.

Eric sat for several minutes with his eyes closed, leaning against the cold metal of the platform railing. Soon, the pain in his skull began to ease, and seeking something to pass the time, Eric returned to the viewing station. Looking through the eyepiece, he realized that the telescope was no longer pointed at Saturn. He wondered how far off the mark it had moved while he and the Professor had been talking. Their conversation had seemed a long one, but Eric had already experienced how easily he could lose track of time in the observatory.

He was sure he could remember the correct sequence the Professor had used when he had first centered the Discovery VII on the ringed planet. Okay, he thought. First look through the large finder scope and put that star in the crosshairs. Eric repeated the instructions to himself as he carried them out. Then adjust these controls under my right hand until Saturn appears in the field of view. Turn this ring for a focus and, bingo! There it is, nice and clear.

Eric was surprised at the overwhelming sense of accomplishment that came over him. It felt good. I'll bet the Professor will be really proud of me, he thought. I remembered everything he did. Eric started to call the Professor's attention to his success when another, more interesting idea occurred to him.

Checking carefully to see if the Professor was still occupied, he located the actuator. While Professor Strang is busy, he thought, I could make the jump back to Saturn. I could be there and home again before he even notices I'm gone. Then he'll *really* be proud of me.

On the other side of the room, the Professor was deep in thought. The interface between the main computer and the Chrysalis was not performing as he had designed it. Something was interfering with the downloading of the data that had been gathered during the mission. Perhaps a new process SID had suggested would be more effective.

"SID, let's regress to the moment of thought transference," he suggested. "Perhaps our inability to download is connected in some way to the translocation itself."

"Right! Do you think that the matter-to-energy procedure is affecting the ship's main computer functions?"

"If that's the case, we'll find out during the replay of the mission."

Professor Strang began to carefully review the readings the computer had recorded from the moment earlier that evening when he had sent Eric to Saturn. Poor boy, he thought. I'll have to learn not to get so wrapped up in what I'm doing while I have visitors. He continued to type in equations as he spoke without turning away from the computer.

"I must apologize once again for becoming so distracted, Eric. I-" The Professor looked up from the workstation just in time to see Eric vanish. Lunging toward the platform, the Professor shouted, "Eric! No!" but he was too late. The boy was gone!

Chapter 12

The Professor's words echoed faintly in Eric's ears as the vortex took him for the second time that evening. The effects of the transfer were far worse than anything he had experienced in his earlier jumps. When he opened his eyes, he was again lying plastered face down on the transparent surface. His head pounded painfully, and when he tried to stand he became dizzy and had to fight to keep the contents of his stomach where they belonged.

I thought the transfer was supposed to get easier each time. If that's the Professor's idea of easier . . . What had he been saying just before I left? It sounded like he'd been shouting, but his words were garbled. Must be another effect of the transfer. I'd better have SID call him and tell him not to worry, Eric thought, but SID was not attached to the computer in the location where he had been earlier. He searched the console from one end to the other, but no SID.

"Hey, SID, where are you? Could you contact Professor Strang and let him know we got here all right?" Eric asked. All was silent. SID was probably waiting for him to ask nicely.

"SID, I said could you send a message, please?" Eric tapped his fingers impatiently. Here we go again, he thought. SID was probably hiding somewhere, sulking.

"SID, would you drop the attitude for a minute? I'd really like to talk to the Professor."

It was eerily quiet inside the bubble. Even the beeps and whirring noises from the computer seemed subdued. Now what do I do, thought Eric. He realized that beyond showing the Professor that he was smart enough to operate his complicated machinery, he really hadn't had any particular plan in coming here. He tried staring out the window for a while, but even though the view was spectacular it was after all, the same view he'd seen on his first trip. It was beginning to get a little tiresome.

"Maybe I should just go back," he said out loud. The volume of his own voice startled him and he laughed nervously. The fact that he seemed to be completely alone, suspended in space over an alien planet had given him an extreme case of the jitters.

But how was he to get back to the observatory? That was an interesting question, one upon which Eric now focused his full attention.

The Professor brought us back last time, thought Eric. And he was in contact with SID the whole time, at least that's what SID told me. But SID's not hiding here aboard the Chrysalis. Eric would feel a lot better if he would just pop out and say, "Ha, ha! Fooled you!" The annoying little database sure picked a bad time to pull a disappearing act. Eric knew he had nothing to worry about, though. The motto inscribed on the Professor's business card had promised that he would remain safe. If he did not believe that, he probably would never have gone to visit the observatory in the first place.

In the meantime, I guess I'll just have to 'hang around' 'til the Professor discovers I'm gone. Eric rolled his eyes at his own feeble joke, and wondered how long that would be.

Maybe I could try out these controls while I wait, thought Eric. He looked over the panel that governed the ship's systems. Some of the labels that SID had explained earlier caught his attention. He read them aloud.

"Hmm, let's see. Environmental readings and life support levels are all green. Green must mean normal. Better not mess with those. Betcha Meredith wouldn't even know what all these lights and gismos are." He did a fair imitation of Meredith's best frown and, pitching his voice a little higher said, "I'm an astronomer, not a starship captain!" He made a face at her in her absence and continued scanning the panel.

"Safety protocols activated," he read. "That wasn't here before. Wonder what it means? Directional Controls. Now here's something! Forward thrusters, aft thrusters, port

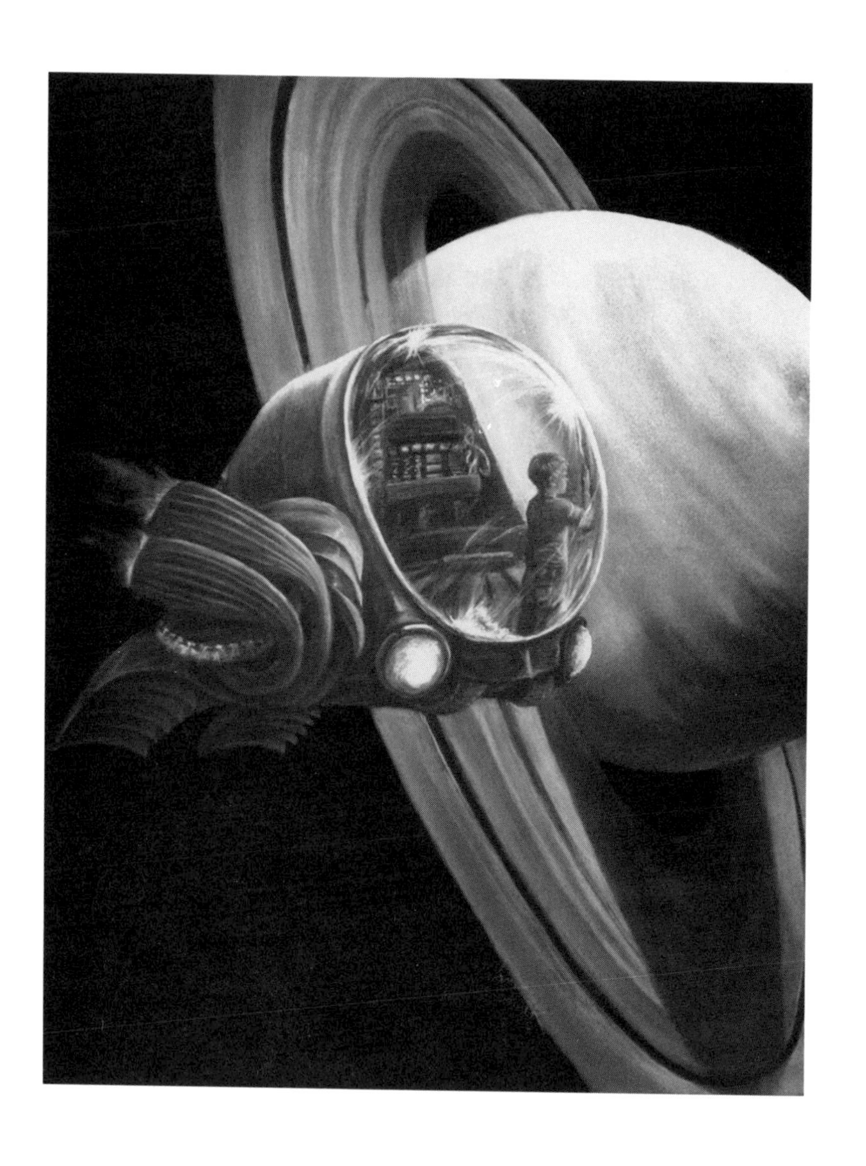

"He was completely alone, suspended over an alien planet."

and starboard – Cool! I could fly the ship!" For a moment Eric considered the possibility that he might damage the craft if he clumsily bumped into something, then he smiled. The Chrysalis is not a car, and I'm not in the Buy & Save parking lot.

"I'm in outer space," he said, "a million miles away from anywhere. What could I hit?"

What should I try first, he thought. He pressed a button under the words 'aft thrusters'. Nothing happened, except that a little green light under 'station keeping' changed to yellow.

"Okay, how about a turn?" Eric knew from SID's explanation that port and starboard meant left and right, but he couldn't remember which meant which. He pressed the port command and was pleased to see another little green light flash. Even before he turned to look at Saturn, he realized that the ship was slowly maneuvering to the left. I always thought piloting a space ship would be hard he thought, but this is a cinch!

He allowed the ship to continue turning until the rings were no longer visible from any part of the Chrysalis' oversized view port. Not even by looking directly between his feet could Eric see anything but Saturn's gigantic planetary sphere. He wasn't sure, but that spot of orange that he had noticed earlier seemed to be getting larger, too.

He turned back to the console and checked the altimeter, which registered the craft's altitude above the surface of the planet. This ship must be moving a lot faster than SID said it did, he thought. Within the last few minutes the reading had changed from 2000 km to 1500 km, and it was still falling.

Eric had some vague idea that he should not allow the Chrysalis to approach the planet too closely, so he shut down the thrusters. The craft's altitude continued to fall. Eric considered this for a moment or two, unsure of the reason until he remembered a part of the discussion they'd had the day Professor Strang had visited them in their classroom.

The topic had been space flight, particularly the conservation of fuel on a long interstellar journey. The discussion had led to the property of inertia and the application of force. An object moving in space would continue to move in the same direction until an opposing force acted on it. That meant that the Chrysalis would keep moving forward until something happened to stop it or change its direction. If unchecked, that forward motion would soon send the tiny spaceship plunging into Saturn's swirling atmosphere.

Suddenly an alarm blared, louder than the fire alarm at school. It had the effect of totally wiping his brain clean. Lights flashed all over the panel. Frantically, Eric searched his mind for one coherent thought to grab on to. If it weren't for that blasted noise. The alarm! That's it! Eric latched on to those two words and, searching the panel, succeeded in finding the command that squelched the warning. What a relief!

Now all I have to do it find out what caused it, he thought. He surveyed the control panel more carefully than before until, just under the altimeter, he found the problem. He wished it had stayed lost. The words PROXIMITY ALERT and DANGER were flashing alternately in bright red letters. The Chrysalis was getting too close to the planet! He had to do something quickly. He keyed the command for aft thrusters, hoping that applying force in the opposite direction would somehow act as a brake for the hurtling spacecraft. Checking the altimeter, he saw that although the speed of his descent had slowed slightly, the ship was still moving toward the planet at incredible speeds.

I must be caught in Saturn's gravity, thought Eric. Now what do I do? He considered adding more power to the thrusters, but he was not sure the craft could take that kind of pressure without breaking apart. He was not sure of anything at this point, least of all his ability to get out of this situation before he turned into a 100 pound slab of bacon! He'd made a terrible mistake thinking he knew enough about the Chrysalis to actually fly it. His first solo space journey was not going as well as he had hoped. In fact, it looked as though it might also be his last!

The air in the cabin was thick. It burned his lungs when he tried to breathe, and the enclosed space was becoming extremely warm. Eric reasoned that as the spaceship lost its battle against the pull of the planet, it must be losing power as well. A dense gray smoke had begun to curl around his feet and rise toward the upper region of the bubble. The smoke carried with it the nose wrinkling reek of burning electronics, a smell he recognized all too well from sixth grade science class. His teacher's experiments had not always gone as planned. Like this trip, he thought. I sure didn't plan for this to happen!

The Professor's going to be really unhappy with me, Eric thought. He trusted me and I wrecked his ship. And what about Mom? What will she think? Eric knew without question that he was in terrible danger. He was going to die out here and she would never know what happened. She'll be all alone!

"It's all my fault!" he whispered faintly. Tears ran down his face, as much from the acrid smoke as from his despair. As he lost consciousness, he thought he could hear the familiar and reassuring sound of Meredith's voice reciting over and over again.

"You're always safe . . . always safe . . . you're always safe with the Professor."

* * * * * * *

All was not going well back in the observatory, either. The Professor knew even before he shouted Eric's name that it was too late. The boy had already made the jump and, impossible as it may seem, he had done it without SID. What a fool he had been to leave Eric alone in the presence of such terrible temptation.

"SID, what happened?" he demanded.

"I don't know," answered the computer, horrified. "I don't know how it happened. I couldn't stop him!"

Without answering, Professor Strang made a few adjustments to the computer, searching determinedly for the information he needed.

"The Chrysalis is no longer at the point of translocation. He must have attempted to pilot the craft manually."

The Professor moved swiftly as he spoke. Running up the ladder to the platform, he snapped SID into his receptacle at the base of the Discovery VII.

"This will make pinpointing his exact location extremely difficult. We must somehow contact the Chrysalis, SID, and determine if there is still a life form reading on board. If Eric's digital information remains in the ship's computer too long, it will degrade and we will never be able to retrieve him."

"I will attempt to triangulate the Chrysalis' position on a tachyon communication link." SID emitted a series of clicking sounds and then was silent for a time.

The Professor prompted him impatiently. "Saturn set is in approximately thirty-seven minutes. We must find him before the planet slips below the horizon."

After more endless seconds ticked by, SID finally announced, "Here he is! The Chrysalis has activated all safety protocols and the boy has been successfully rematerialized through the ship's processor. Quite a bit more uncomfortable than when I do it . . . I'll bet he's got a whopping headache."

"We don't have time for this, SID," snapped the Professor. "Where is he?"

"Your assistant is very predictable," SID said, not unkindly. "He has returned to Saturn."

"Not so predictable as I might have wished."

"Not so predictable as a computer," sniffed SID, "although I am at a loss to explain this entire situation."

"Examine your recordings of the past two minutes," the Professor suggested.

"Yes, sir." SID's voice trembled anxiously.

As he waited, the Professor's thoughts raced. Without SID aboard the Chrysalis, Eric had no way to return. The space craft had the capability to wallow about in Saturn's atmosphere for a short time, but it would soon crash to the planet's surface if SID was not there to convert its mass to digital energy and then attach it to the return tachyon beam.

SID broke into the Professor's thoughts. "Professor, I have examined the recordings as you requested, and I believe I have discovered the problem. When I replayed the data from the first translocation, the information 'felt' thicker, almost fuzzy. I thought this was the download problem we were looking for but it was really the result of an overlap. The readings caused by Eric readying the telescope for this jump were identical to the data from the original translocation, except for a slight time delay. The rebounding echo effect that resulted made it nearly impossible to distinguish the second event from the first. The chances of this happening are 1,785, 432 to one. I gave the green light to send Eric to Saturn because I thought it was just a simulation, while he was pressing the actuator in real time. It was my fault, Professor."

"Nonsense, SID. You must be in the ACT Receptacle for the translocation to work!"

"Evidently not," replied SID. "I have always been in the receptacle for every trip we have attempted. We never considered it could be done any differently. But I cannot bring him back from here. I must be in close proximity to Eric and the Chrysalis in order to complete the transference. How are we going to bring them home?"

"You've got to get out there, SID."

"And just how do you propose I get there?"

The Professor was silent for so long that SID began to suspect that he had no answer to the question.

"You will have to take me there yourself," the computer suggested.

"You know I can't do that, as much as I might want to," the Professor snapped sharply. "Someone must remain in the observatory to monitor and control the return tachyon beam. It's too unstable."

"What about the girl?" asked SID.

"Meredith? Don't be ridiculous. I agree the child is unusually bright, but she could never learn the Discovery's systems in time."

"No, Professor. That is not what I meant. Send me with her to the Chrysalis."

"What? And risk more lives? You must be mad!"

Professor Strang put his head in his hands. It was not a gesture of defeat however, only an attempt to think things through more clearly. Quiet filled the room.

"Sir, I'm sorry to disturb you, but I'm detecting a faint but alarming echo from the Chrysalis' computer. Her orbit is decaying and life support seems to be malfunctioning. You will have to make a decision now!"

The Professor stood with a grave expression on his lined face.

"I already have. Continue monitoring ship's functions. On your very life SID, you must not lose her. I'll be back soon."

"Where are you going?" called SID.

The Professor was halfway down the stairs, but his answer drifted back to SID on the cold night air.

"To get help!" he said, and then he was gone.

Chapter 13

It was only a short drive to the Weatherford's home, but it gave the Professor time to think. Almost immediately he was overcome with blame; blame for sending Eric through the telescope in the first place, blame for leaving him alone with the device and now, blame for what he was about to ask of a young girl to whom he had never been properly introduced. But no matter how much guilt he heaped upon himself, he could think of no other way to save Eric.

He must make all haste to convince Mr. and Mrs. Weatherford that their daughter's presence was needed at the observatory without alerting them to his desperate situation. That would not be easy, but harder still would be convincing Meredith to trust him. Trust would not come easy to the girl. She was a true scientist, believing only in what she could see with her eyes and in what she could prove with her intellect. Yet without trust, the incredible systems of the Discovery would be powerless. If I fail to earn Meredith's confidence, he thought, *I* will be powerless to bring Eric home.

As he took long strides up the sidewalk, Professor Strang began to breathe deeply, a technique he had used to calm himself before giving lectures during his early days at the university. The trick failed to work in this instance and when Mr. Weatherford answered his knock, he was afraid that the man would be able to hear his heart hammering against his chest. He was surprised by the steadiness in his voice as he spoke.

"Good evening, Mr. Weatherford. I was wondering if I might have a moment of your time."

"Well, Dr. Strang, how nice of you to stop by!" Meredith's father reached out to shake the Professor's hand, and at the same time drew him into the entryway. "Won't you come in?"

Mr. Weatherford ushered his guest into the family's living room, where they were watching television. Meredith looked up and gasped in surprise. She had not seen the strange man since that day in the classroom, and having him abruptly appear in her own living room was like finding a diamond ring as a prize in a box of cereal; it just didn't fit.

He smiled at her. She returned the smile hesitantly.

"This is my wife, Monica," said Mr. Weatherford. "And, of course, you already know Meredith."

"Please sit down, won't you?" asked Mrs. Weatherford, indicating a place on the sofa.

"No, thank you. Actually, I am rather in a hurry, Mrs. Weatherford. You see, I was hoping to ask a favor. Young Mr. Spencer and I are in the middle of some research at the observatory and we only have a short time window in which to complete our experiments. I was wondering if I might enlist the help of your daughter? A third person at this point would be of great assistance."

Meredith's smile widened. Was she finally going to get a look through the Professor's scope? She crossed her fingers behind her back, hoping her dad would let her go. He seemed to read her mind, for he said, "That would be fine. We would have let her come over with Eric earlier tonight, but she had some chores she had to finish." Mr. Weatherford smiled craftily at his own use of the word 'chores'. "Would you like to go, honey? You could ask Eric's mother for a ride home. "

"Sure, Dad, if it's okay with you and Mom." She held her breath.

"Well, get your coat then. Let's not keep the man waiting."

Meredith ran to the closet and grabbed her coat off the hanger. Her father went to the desk and handed the Professor the long envelope that contained Meredith's permission form.

"I'm sorry it's taken us so long to get Meredith to the viewing sessions."

"That's perfectly all right, Mr. Weatherford," said the Professor with a forced calmness, "the sky will always be there. My plan is to have open sessions all summer long.

We have all the time in the world." As he led Meredith outside to his car and opened the door for her, he found himself wishing with all his might that it were true.

Once they were on their way, Meredith immediately sensed an abrupt change in the Professor's mood. She wasted no words on politeness.

"Something's happened to Eric," she said.

Professor Strang kept his eyes on the road, but nodded.

"When Eric told you that he had traveled to the Andromeda Galaxy, did you believe it was true?"

"Not at first," she answered.

"What caused you to change your mind?"

"Eric did. I trust him, so I had to believe him."

The Professor pounced on her answer like a hungry tiger. "And that, my dear, will save your friend's life!"

"What do you mean? What have you done to Eric?" she demanded. He ignored her question and began to explain.

"Time is short, and I have much to tell you. You must listen as if your life depended upon it. Eric's life does." He first informed her of the existence of the Discovery VII and its ability, with SID's help, to transport a person to any location in the universe. Then he briefly told her of the short research mission he had sent the boy and SID on earlier that evening.

"Who is SID?" she asked.

"SID is an interactive database. He is able to intercept human brain waves, convert them to digital information, then attach them to a tachyon beam and execute the translocation process aboard the Chrysalis; a cosmosphere that accepts its commands directly from the Discovery VII. The operator chooses the location, centers the telescope upon it as in normal viewing, and then sends a signal to SID to begin the transference. However, SID must be physically connected to the telescope's main computer in an Amplified Conversion Transponder Receptacle, and within five hundred feet of the user."

"Something's happened to Eric!"

"So what went wrong?" she asked.

"SID was assisting me in another part of the observatory and was not connected to the ACT at the time. Eric jumped before either the computer or I were aware of his intent, and so made the transference without the means to return. I was not aware until this very evening that the translocation procedure could be completed with the interactive device disconnected from the computer. I did not even consider that it was possible. Logically, I assumed that anyone using the Discovery would do so under my direct supervision. I assumed wrong and, as a result, this has become a rescue mission."

"A rescue mission?" she squeaked.

"Without SID along, Eric cannot return from Saturn."

"Couldn't you stop him?"

The Professor shook his head. "The process is instantaneous. By the time SID and I realized our error, it was too late." He sighed. "I failed to consider the boy's intellect, not to mention his unbounded curiosity. In short, I underestimated him."

"Don't feel bad, I do that all the time," said Meredith.

"And what is the usual result?"

"Utter chaos," admitted the girl. "But, you know, on the outside, Eric seems so -."

"Commonplace?"

"Yes. While on the inside, he's very –"

"Extraordinary." Once again, the Professor finished her sentence for her.

"Actually, I was about to say special," she said, frowning. "That's a really annoying habit, by the way."

"What is?"

"Finishing other people's sentences," she answered. "Do you do it often?"

"More or less."

"Now I know why my parents dislike it so much!" She turned in her seat. "So what do we do now?"

"Someone must travel through the telescope with SID so that he can re-connect with the computer aboard the Chrysalis and bring her home. And quickly, before Saturn sets."

"And if Saturn sets before we're able to do that?"

"We'll lose him," said the Professor dismally.

She looked out the car window to locate Saturn in the western sky. "We don't have much time," she said.

The Professor consulted his watch. "Only twenty-one minutes. But we have an even more pressing problem. Something has happened to the ship. We believe that she is caught in Saturn's gravitational pull and is losing altitude at an alarming rate. Soon life support will begin to malfunction as the ship loses power."

"And you're asking me to . . . ?"

"I know of no one better fitted for this assignment than you," he answered.

"Me? Why me? Why not you, or – or some other grown up person who knows what they're doing?"

"Most adults find it impossible to travel by means of thought transference. I would gladly go, however someone must remain behind to monitor the return tachyon beam. I'm afraid it would take many weeks to instruct you in all that you would need to know. As for other adults, David and I are the only ones who are familiar with the workings of the Discovery VII."

"Who is David?" asked Meredith.

Embarrassed that he had let slip such a private thought, the Professor paused for a moment before answering. His face seemed to age before her eyes.

"David is my son."

"Great!" she said with a sigh of relief. "Then he can go rescue Eric."

"I'm afraid that would be quite impossible. He died a few years ago when he was just sixteen." The Professor spoke so quietly that Meredith had to strain to hear him.

"I'm so sorry!" Meredith felt awful. She hadn't meant to hurt the Professor with all her questions. Suddenly she stopped short.

"Wait a minute. Your son didn't –"

The Professor knew immediately what the girl was thinking. "David's death had nothing to do with the telescope." He took his eyes off the road for a moment to look at her. Her sympathetic gaze cut him like a knife.

"No, Meredith. The telescope did not kill my son," he repeated emphatically. "In fact, it gave him a reason to go on living for a few days, a few weeks longer. But I will not deceive you, young lady, traveling at the speed of thought is not completely without risks."

"Risks?" asked Meredith in a shaky voice.

"The Chrysalis may be damaged. I have never attempted translocation with the cosmosphere already in space, not to mention carrying two life forms at the same time. And there is one other complication."

Meredith wasn't sure she could deal with any more 'complications'. Although the Professor's story was perfectly in line with everything Eric had tried to tell her, the facts were still slipping and sliding through the scientific cogs of her mind.

She had to ask. "What kind of complications?"

"Thought travel depends upon complete and utter faith in the telescope and its ability to convey you to any location in the universe. The human mind has many pathways. In the mind of a child those pathways are straight and uncluttered, but as the child matures and the experiences of life accumulate, many twists and turns develop. Walls are erected to protect the psyche from harmful thoughts and feelings. These walls are difficult to penetrate. Understandably then, the only minds that are open to the possibilities of travel through interstellar space in this way are children and very imaginative adults. I waited until the moment I felt that your friend Eric trusted me completely before I sent him on his long journey. And now, in order to use the telescope and save your friend, you must trust me, too."

"But, how can I?" Meredith blurted out.

"Indeed, how can you? How could you be expected to believe in someone that you don't even know? Especially someone who has behaved as strangely as I have? And who has put your friend in such jeopardy!" The Professor seemed as though he was speaking more to himself than to his passenger. Then he asked her for the second time that evening, "Do you trust Eric?"

"Yes!" Meredith answered immediately. She had already settled that question in her own mind and knew that her answer was the opening of a great door; a door that would lead her out of her world of reason and into a future filled with magical possibilities.

"I hope that will be enough," said the Professor bleakly. He haphazardly parked the car, not caring that its nose was half buried in the shrubbery that lined the driveway. As they crossed the few feet to the front door, Meredith followed the Professor's fear-filled gaze to the sky, where the ghostly glow of Saturn could be seen just inches from the western horizon.

"We must hurry," urged the Professor.

Had it been under other circumstances, her curiosity about the man would have caused her to look around carefully as she followed him through the dark house, but now her thoughts were only for Eric and for what was about to happen to him. She felt a great twisting in her mid-section, as though a giant spring of excitement were coiling tightly inside her.

She was going to travel through space! No rational human being could believe it was even possible to take the kind of leap the Professor had described. But she must accept it, or Eric would die! What was it that Professor Strang had said? Traveling at the speed of thought. She had heard of scientists who had experimented with technology that would enable an object to be transported from one place to another on a beam of light. So far as she knew, none of their trials had met with success. But thought transference! Could it really work?

Her questions would have to wait, for none of their answers would help her at all in the task that lay before her. No amount of information in the world would prevent her reasonable mind from being skeptical about any idea or theory she had not thoroughly tried and tested herself. Yet now, if what the Professor had told her was true, Eric's life depended on her ability to make a leap of faith! If she had not been so frightened, she might have laughed out loud at her predicament.

The urge to laugh left her completely as she entered the observatory. She even forgot her fright. She forgot everything as she looked up at the giant telescope for the first time. It seemed to hang suspended in the chill air as if gravity had no effect on it. It was big and bright and beautiful! The adjectives kept filling her head. Oh, to be allowed to gaze and gaze at any object she pleased! To spend the dark hours of the night exploring the universe!

Her thoughts were interrupted as the Professor urgently pressed something into her hand. It looked like her dad's television remote that he was always misplacing somewhere around the house.

"This is SID," said the Professor.

"Let's skip the introductions for now and get a move on," said the database.

It was a good thing that the Professor still held the girl's hand, for SID would have taken a short flight of his own when Meredith jumped in surprise at his unexpected words. Professor Strang appeared not to have noticed, for he put his arm about Meredith's shoulders and led her toward the telescope.

"Normally, you would travel inside the Chrysalis to a position just outside of Saturn's major gravitational influence. However, because the Chrysalis is already orbiting Saturn, SID will take you directly to its present location." As he spoke, he guided Meredith's hand which still clutched SID's small form to the interface at the base of the telescope. He snapped the database into position and pressed her fingers tightly around it.

"We have never attempted a jump like this, so I want you to maintain actual physical contact with SID until you have safely reached your destination. As soon as you arrive he will begin to evaluate the status of the Chrysalis and make the corrections necessary to return her to a stationary orbit around Saturn."

"What should I do?" asked Meredith.

"SID will inform you if he needs your assistance. Otherwise, see to Eric. If the ship has encountered turbulence, he may be injured. As soon as you have reached station keeping orbit, I will send the return tachyon beam for you and SID can bring you home."

"Professor?" Meredith turned to him, her eyes wide. "What if . . .?"

"Fourteen minutes, 32 seconds," broke in SID. Then, very quietly, he added, "C'mon, Meredith. We can do this. Trust me." At that moment, he sounded more like a boy than a computer database. He sounded like Eric!

The tears that had gathered squeezed out from behind her tightly closed eyes as she nodded determinedly. "All right, let's go."

"Whenever you're ready, SID" said the Professor. "Look in the eyepiece, Meredith. And hang on! According to Eric, you're in for a bumpy ride!"

No sooner had she focused her eyes on Saturn, than it began to grow larger until it filled the eyepiece, and she felt herself falling into the black emptiness of space.

Chapter 14

As if from a terrible nightmare, Meredith awoke to swirling black smoke and nauseating pain that reverberated from her skull bones to the base of her spine. She couldn't remember ever experiencing such blinding agony. She was slumped over a computer console of some kind, SID still gripped tightly in her hand.

"SID, are you all right?" she choked out frantically.

"I am fine," he answered. "I am accessing the main computer. The damage to the ship's systems is extensive."

"Where's Eric?"

"I'm not sure."

"I've got to find him!"

"We will, but not until we clear the air in here. I will bring the Chrysalis back to the point of translocation. We can't jump from here. Your first priority is to recycle the ship's oxygen. Environmental controls are to your right."

Meredith peered through the dim murkiness. The pain in her head had not lessened one bit, but her vision had begun to clear and as she found and adjusted the appropriate controls, she became aware of a mechanical whining sound, high pitched and growing steadily louder. The throbbing in her brain grew into a gigantic, mind numbing torture.

"What's that noise?"

"The Chrysalis is caught in the planet's considerable gravity. I am using her engines well past their capacity in an attempt to pull us away."

Realizing that she could do nothing further to help SID, she dropped back to the floor and began to search for Eric. The smoke was less dense here, and for the first time she could see through the transparent surface to the planet that was dragging them toward it, beautiful in its terrible closeness! How often she had admired it. It was always the first planet she looked for in the evening sky. It's ironic, she thought, that Saturn, so many millions of miles from Earth, might be the last sight I'll ever see.

Finally, her hand touched something soft and moist. And hot! Terribly hot! Eric! He was lying motionless, face down. Oh, no! Was she too late? She felt for a pulse but could find none. She couldn't even tell if he was breathing. She berated herself harshly for never having taken a CPR or First Aid course of any kind.

"Eric, wake up!" She shook him gently. "Eric!" She was afraid to shake him any harder, in case he might be injured in some way she couldn't see. Carefully rolling him onto his back she placed her ear against his mouth in an attempt to catch the slightest movement of air, but the continued din from the engines kept her from hearing any sound of life from her friend. Finally she sat beside him helplessly.

"Eric, please!" she cried. "Don't leave me! SID!" Her voice was so choked with the black smoke that she could barely hear it herself. She called again, louder.

"SID! Help me!" There was no answer from the computer. SID was too busy to respond. She noticed that the smoke was beginning to clear and when she looked back at Eric's face, she started in surprise. His eyes were open and he was staring up at her, frowning at her actually!

"What are you doing here?" His voice was a croaking whisper.

"Eric! You're alive!" She hugged him fiercely.

"Am I?" he asked. "I was beginning to wonder . . ." He tightened his arms around her briefly and then released her, peering at her face through her tangled, unbraided hair.

"Why are you crying?" he asked.

She did not answer, but wiped her eyes with her hands. He sat up shakily and put his head on his knees.

"I don't feel so good."

"You don't look so good either." He looked up at her as she knelt beside him. She pulled out a corner of her T-shirt and began to mop his face with it. The grime came off in big smears, showing patches of deathly pale skin underneath.

"Eric, wake up!"

"Thanks," he said.

The air was becoming much clearer now, and he looked around him, still groggy and bewildered by her presence.

"Are we still on the ship? Is the Professor here?"

"He's back at the observatory. But SID is here, now. He's trying to get us back on course."

"SID's here?" Suddenly Eric came fully to his senses and remembered the danger they were in. He tried to get to his knees but was held back by Meredith's firm hands on his shoulders.

"You've got to get out of here! This ship is going to crash into the planet!"

"Not if I can help it," said SID.

"SID, call the Professor! We've got to get Meredith out of here before we crash." Eric struggled to get to his feet, but in his present condition, Meredith was more than a match for him. He remained on the floor, where the air was now becoming quite clean and breathable.

"Shut up, Eric," said Meredith. "We're here to rescue you. The Professor promised he'd bring you home safely, remember?"

"You don't understand! It's too late!" Eric's mind was still tangled in panic.

"Calm down, boy. I have everything perfectly under control. Two minutes to orbit," SID informed them.

Meredith sat on the floor next to Eric. He was breathing much easier since the air inside the craft had been completely recycled. He had stopped turning wildly from side to side, and had resigned himself to awaiting their fate quietly. Now that she was sure Eric was out of immediate danger, Meredith turned her attention back to the amazing sight outside the bubble.

The ship's engines, although still struggling, were quieter now. They were passing between the rings of Saturn. Above them and below them she could see the beautiful bands of colored rock and ice. The sight of the gas giant held her enthralled in a dreamlike trance for several seconds. Unbelievable! Meredith wished she could sit there forever, suspended outside of time.

"Time!" she said, startled. "How much do we have, SID?"

"Four minutes, eleven seconds to Saturn set," he answered.

"We're cutting it pretty close, aren't we?" she asked.

"I'm pushing the engines to their top capacity. They have sustained considerable damage."

Eric thought SID was being extremely kind not mentioning who had done the damaging.

"Is there anything I can do to help?" he asked.

"No, thank you. You have helped quite enough today," SID answered.

So much for kindness! Eric stretched his legs stiffly and wondered if they would hold him up now. Meredith helped him to his feet and he took a few trembling steps on his own.

"Orbit in five, four, three, two, one," said SID. There was a slight pause and then, "I am now in contact with Professor Strang. He sends his greetings and suggests that we move with great haste. Meredith, would you assist Eric?"

Assist him with what, she thought, and then she understood as the padded chair appeared. Against protests from Eric, she pushed him into the seat and pulled the straps out of his still shaking hands to buckle him in. She did not know why, but at this moment his closeness embarrassed her and she avoided his eyes.

He grabbed clumsily at her hand and caught it in his. She let go of the belt for a moment and looked directly at him. He gave her a grateful smile.

"You okay?"

"Yeah, except for this awful headache. It won't go away."

"It's the transfer. I can't really explain it, but I think it has something to do with SID being inside your brain, rearranging things."

"Oh, now that makes me feel a whole lot better," she said sarcastically.

"I'm really sorry I got us into this," he said.

"Its okay, Eric," she said. "I would have done the same thing."

"Yeah, but you wouldn't have messed it up like I did. SID was right. The Professor should have gotten someone else. He should have picked you."

She gave the belt a tug, making sure it was secure. Then she sat down in the next safest place she could find; on the floor beside him.

"He did pick me. I'm here, aren't I?" As usual, her logic left him without reply. She entwined her arms around the harness that held Eric in his seat and held on tight.

"SID," she raised her voice so the computer could hear. "We're ready. Let's go home."

"Yes, let's!" agreed the computer brightly.

* * * * * * *

As soon as Meredith and SID had gone, Professor Strang wandered restlessly to the main computer where he tried again and again to call the Chrysalis, without success. She must truly be lost somewhere amidst the rings of Saturn. SID would not be able to contact him until he had pulled the craft back into a station keeping orbit; back to the point of transference.

The Professor sank wearily into a chair. Suddenly he felt very old. If he had been a nervous person, he would have quickly worn a path between the worktable and the computer by anxiously pacing back and forth, but he was not a pacer. Instead, he chose to spend the endless minutes sitting quietly, gazing at the oversized photographs on the walls of the observatory.

Alone, without even the company of his computerized companion, the harsh words of blame that he had been forced to hold back until now began to fall upon him like bricks. I never should have sent Eric through the

"Alone ... blame began to fall upon him like a ton of bricks."

telescope . . . he wasn't ready. . . I thought I knew him better, he's so much like me . . . I assumed he knew more . . . I just didn't prepare him well enough. Why did I let this happen?

A small voice inside his head was insistently telling him that it was too late to save Eric, just like it had been too late to save David. He had been so wrapped up in his research at the time that he had not even noticed that his only son was keeping a terrible secret carefully hidden from his father. By the time the doctors had discovered the cancer, it had spread throughout his entire system. No power on earth or in space had been able save him then.

After David's death, he had buried himself in the observatory, in the hope that he could forget his pain; forget the longing he felt for his lost boy. For a time his plan had worked. Long hours of experiments in his laboratory had allowed him to sink into sleep each night like a dead man with no hope of resurrection. Yet every morning he awoke again with the realization that the one person with whom he could share his triumph, his joy of discovery, was forever beyond his reach.

David had taken such pleasure in trading places with him, taking turns jumping from world to world in the Chrysalis, and then remaining behind for safety's sake so that his father could jump as well. But the impossible dream that he and David had shared together had ended too soon. Without the uncluttered mind of a child for SID to tap into, the Discovery VII sat idle and gathered dust. The Professor did not have the heart to look through the telescope, even for ordinary stargazing, for there would be no more journeys to the Orion Nebula, no more nightly jaunts around the moons of Jupiter and back. For three years, the Professor's life had been one full of regrets and memories that he had tried unsuccessfully to push away.

And then Eric and Meredith had come along. It was SID's idea, actually. He and the Professor had been talking one afternoon, reliving their travels aboard the Chrysalis. SID had suggested that the Professor go to the university and find some promising young Astronomy student to train up as an apprentice. At first the idea had been totally alien to him. Imagine the disloyalty of trying to find someone to take David's place! And it would also have to be someone that the Professor could trust with the incredible secret of the Discovery VII's existence and its capabilities.

The astronomical world had scoffed when he had first broached the idea of space travel through a telescope, especially when it appeared that only children could use it. What good were children in space? The greatest scientists on the planet were unable to grasp that the key to space exploration lay in the simplicity of a child's mind. They said it was impossible, they had taken away his research grants, but he had found private funding to continue his life work.

The further he pursued his research, however, the more he realized the potential for misuse was enormous. If the telescope was to fall into greedy hands, imagine the devastation of as yet undiscovered worlds, stripped of their ores and precious metals. Why, the knowledge of SID's artificial intelligence alone, put in the hands of a terrorist government, could be disastrous. An unscrupulous person could twist the computer's intricate technology to create a weapon that could invade the privacy of the human mind.

There seemed to be so many obstacles standing between him and the fulfillment of his dreams that the Professor found himself on the verge of giving up entirely. After a time though, and much encouragement from his digitalized assistant, he had begun to seriously consider the idea of finding an apprentice. But not a university student. The person he chose must have a younger mind, one that was wide open to the possibilities of space travel. Thought transference was only successful if a person could open his mind to the device and its creator completely; that would eliminate a large percentage of Earth's population.

While the Professor was willing to admit that SID's idea had merit, he was sure that he would never find someone with the right qualities. But if he did . . . how wonderful it would be to journey to the stars once again!

When his friend Jim Kincaid asked him to speak at his school's Career Day, he never imagined he would find the two perfect candidates practically under his nose! Two teenagers!

SID had been with him that day, tucked away safely in the pocket of his lab coat. It had not taken long for the computer to scan every adolescent mind in the school. The Professor could recall SID's excitement when, just before entering the classroom for that final Astronomy session, he recognized their future apprentice. Meredith Weatherford. When the Professor had scanned the student's faces it was easy to single her out as she sat in the third row. Yet another face caught his attention; a face that had a very familiar expression upon it, an expression very much like the one he saw each morning in the mirror.

What was it about the boy that made him special? SID had not singled him out or noticed him in any way, yet the Professor was sure that this young man had the potential to become more than an astronomer. He was a dreamer, like David.

SID had pitched a fit. Eric did not fit the profile; he was not the person they were looking for. The Professor had been insistent, though, that both the children be tested. So using the same thought transference process that operated the Discovery VII, SID animated the pictures for only Meredith and Eric to see. And see they did!

Suddenly he heard a noise, faint and far away, that brought him back to the present. He leaned closer to the computer to listen. It was SID! What was he saying?

" . . our, three, two, one. Station keeping. Professor Strang, are you reading me?"

"Loud and clear, SID. Is everyone all right?"

"Yes. Shaken up a bit, but none the worse for the wear."

"Thank goodness!" Like cobwebs from an ancient attic ceiling, the anxious frown fell from his face as he wiped at it with both hands. Thank goodness, they're all right, he thought.

"How's the Chrysalis?"

"Not so good, Professor. Life support is functioning at forty-six percent for now. I suggest you transmit the return tachyon beam as soon as possible."

"Are the children ready?"

"As ready as they can be," answered the computer.

"Bring them home, SID. Transmitting now."

Chapter 15

As if from nowhere, the two children appeared on the platform. Meredith was supporting Eric, helping him down the ladder. When Eric looked up and saw a familiar tall form emerge from the darkness, he launched himself from the bottom step and landed in the Professor's unsuspecting arms. Eric clung to him tightly, while Meredith watched quietly from the steps. The Professor, uncomfortable with the tempest of the boy's emotions, stood stiffly waiting for them to subside.

Finally Eric spoke, his voice muffled in the Professor's shirt. "Professor, I – I'm so sorry." He looked up into his mentor's careworn face with eyes that were red and swollen. Tears were wearing a path down his sooty, stained cheeks.

"I didn't know! I didn't mean to - ," he broke off lamely and buried his face again.

"Here, now," said the Professor. "It's not your fault."

He firmly but gently pushed Eric from him, and stooped to meet the boy eye to eye.

"You have done nothing wrong, Eric. It is I that should apologize once again. I should never have become so wrapped up in what I was doing. It's perfectly understandable that your curiosity would get the better of you."

"But Professor," explained Eric. "I put Meredith in danger, and SID. And - and I wrecked the Chrysalis!"

"I'm fine, Eric, so you can stop worrying on that score," said Meredith.

"Pardon me, but the danger was minimal. I had everything under control," said SID.

"SID! Are you okay?" asked Eric.

"I'm fine. I am perfectly capable of taking care of myself, and any less intelligent beings present."

"SID," protested Meredith. "Can't you give Eric a break? He's had a hard day!"

The Professor smiled and beckoned to Meredith, encouraging her to join them.

"I agree," he said. "Give it a rest, SID."

Eric didn't mind SID's sarcastic tone. He was just relieved that the little computer had not been damaged. Now he was ready to withstand any amount of teasing his digital friend wanted to dish out. In a way he was glad that SID refused to cut him any slack. He needed someone around to remind him never to pull a stupid stunt like that again.

"No, Professor. SID's right. What I did today was really dumb, and when I think of what could have happened to Meredith . . ."

Until now, Eric had been leaning against the Professor, supported partly by his strong arm and partly by the stair railing, but as he turned to face his friend he stumbled and nearly fell. Meredith caught him and with the Professor's help they half dragged, half carried him to the couch.

Against Eric's protests, Meredith removed his shoes and covered him with a quilt that lay over the back of the couch.

"SID," said the Professor. "Could you please close the dome? And raise the lights a little."

Meredith watched, fascinated as the white dome of the observatory began to close silently. The room quickly began to get warmer.

"SID," the Professor said quietly in a concerned voice. "We need to run a full medical scan on both of the children, specifically for smoke inhalation as well as CO2 and monoxide levels."

"Scanning, Professor," replied the computer. "This won't hurt a bit." He made a few short beeping sounds and columns of numbers appeared on his display screen. "CO2 levels are normal," he continued. "Monoxide levels are elevated, but within safe limits. Their throats will be a little sore and they may wish to limit strenuous physical activity for a day or two, but currently there is no need for medical attention."

"What, no marathon tomorrow?" joked Meredith.

Relieved, the Professor asked, "Miss Weatherford, would you mind making us all something to drink – hot chocolate perhaps?" the Professor asked her. "Take SID down to the kitchen and he'll show you where everything is."

"Sure. C'mon SID." She retrieved the database from his receptacle and disappeared down the stairs.

The Professor drew up a chair to sit near where Eric lay with his eyes closed. It looked as though the boy had fallen asleep. I certainly wouldn't blame him thought the Professor, with all I've put him through this evening. He examined the young face carefully. It was extremely pale beneath the dirt and grime.

A few moments later, SID and Meredith returned with a loaded tray of crackers, cheese, cookies, and the asked for hot chocolate, steaming fragrantly from large brown mugs. She set the tray on the worktable silently, for she sensed that the Professor was lost in thought and she did not want to disturb him.

He was sitting with his elbows on his knees, his head resting in both hands. It was an attitude of defeat. Until now, she had only seen the dynamic side of his personality; constantly in motion, excited, energized by his zeal for his chosen subject. But here was a different man; withdrawn and reserved. This is the first time I've seen him sit still, Meredith thought. He looks lost. She didn't know why, but the thought saddened her.

To dispel the sense of gloom she felt, she picked up the tray and allowed the cups to rattle together. Professor Strang leaped up to help her, pulling a small table to a convenient location near the couch. If he was embarrassed to be caught in such a vulnerable pose, he did not show it.

"I raided your refrigerator," she explained. "I hope you don't mind."

"Of course not," he said.

Meredith sat beside Eric and jiggled him until he awoke.

"Food's here. Are you hungry?"

He opened his eyes, blinking against the light.

"Yeah, I guess I am." He reached for a mug and used its heat to warm his hands. Meredith offered another mug to the Professor.

"Thank you." He wrinkled his nose as she passed near him.

"You could both do with a wash," he said.

"That's a great idea," said Meredith. "But what about our clothes?" It was a sure thing they couldn't go home smelling like this.

"Hmm." Professor Strang considered their problem. "I think it might work." He seemed to be talking more to himself than to either of them. "Finish your snack, and then meet us at the bottom of the stairs." He and SID left the room deep in conversation.

Meredith watched Professor Strang retreat with raised eyebrows. "He's being mysterious again," she said.

"Again?" offered Eric, "when did he stop?"

She giggled, finished the cracker sandwich she was eating, and pulled at Eric's jacket.

"Can you get up, or do I have to carry you?" she asked.

"I can get up." He threw off the blanket and stood up. His legs were still a bit shaky but on the whole, he felt much better after his little nap and the snack she'd fed him.

The Professor met them at the bottom of the stairs and led them down a hallway they hadn't noticed before. Opening a door to his left, they entered a chamber that had absolutely no resemblance to any room in any house they had ever seen. It was about the size of a small bathroom. In fact, evidence remained that it had once been a bathroom, but now the familiar fixtures were replaced by a large control panel. Hanging along the wall were several of the Professor's ultra bright, white lab coats.

"This is the entrance to my clean room," said the Professor.

"You have a clean room in your house?" asked Meredith incredulously.

"Of course." The man's tone was matter of fact, as though having a clean room was a normal occurrence in everyone's home.

"What's a clean room?" asked Eric, feeling entirely left out.

Meredith explained. "It's a place that is free from dust particles and bacteria, where scientific experiments can be carried out without contamination."

"Very good, Miss Weatherford."

"May we see it?" she asked hopefully.

"Not tonight. The contents of that room will have to wait for another time. However, we can make use of this decontamination chamber."

Eric looked around, frantically wondering what new and even weirder experience was coming his way next. Once again Professor Strang seemed able to read his mind for he chuckled and said, "Don't worry Eric. Nothing more is going to happen to you tonight. Commence decontamination," he ordered the computer.

The room filled with a dense mist that swirled about them like fog on a cool autumn morning. Eric instinctively held his breath.

"Breathe normally, children. The mist will not harm you," said the Professor.

"Is this chamber like the one the astronauts used when they returned from the Apollo missions to the moon?" asked Meredith.

"Somewhat," answered the Professor, "although I have made a few special adaptations of my own."

Why doesn't that surprise me, thought Eric. Once he realized he was in no danger, he relaxed and peered through the mist. With astonishment, he saw that the dirt and dust that had covered Meredith's face and clothing was vanishing along with the strange fog.

"Hey, look!" he said, and held up his own sleeve to be examined. "I'm clean."

"And so am I!" Meredith touched Eric's face lightly where a large welt had formed. Covered by dirt, it had gone unnoticed until now.

"How're you going to explain that?" she asked.

"Oh, that's easy," he replied sheepishly. "I did that before I ever went aboard the Chrysalis. I fell against the railing."

"Smooth. Very smooth," she teased him.

"Well, it moves you know!"

The Professor had been listening to their discussion with his head bowed. When the mist finally cleared, he shouldered past them to re-set the chamber controls, no longer able to hide his amusement. He was extremely relieved that the boy was feeling better.

"He's laughing at us!" Eric exclaimed. "Can you believe that?"

"It sounds like laughter, yes. But you're wrong about one thing," she said.

"What's that?" asked Eric.

"He's laughing at you!" She had been combing out her clean hair through her fingers and now she flung it back over her shoulder in her same old way that he knew so well. He was glad she was acting normally toward him again. That 'glass about to break' treatment she'd been giving him earlier had made him feel creepy.

When the last wisps of mist had disappeared along with the dirt on their clothes, the Professor opened the same door they had entered and politely motioned for them to lead the way back up the stairs.

"I'll be along in a moment," he told them.

"Wow! A clean room," Meredith said under her breath, "and a decon chamber. The Professor must be loaded!"

"Yeah," agreed Eric. "I'll bet he saves a lot on laundry, anyway."

Meredith smacked his shoulder playfully. She, too, was glad to have Eric back to his old self.

In the observatory once more, they returned to the couch and their snacks. Their hot chocolate had grown cold long ago but the children didn't mind, for with the dome closed the room was now as warm as the rest of the house. The Professor and SID had rejoined them, but were conferring in another part of the room out of earshot.

"Are you okay, Eric?" Meredith asked. She passed him the plate of snacks and he took a large handful of crackers and some cheese.

"Mmm hmm," he mumbled with his mouth full. "I am now. How 'bout you?" His words came out generously laced with crumbs. She brushed them away without comment.

"My head still hurts like crazy. Do you think SID scrambled my brain or something?"

"How could we tell?"

"Don't be smart!"

"You know I didn't mean it that way. How can we tell that we're not changed somehow?"

"Of course we're changed. We've just been to Saturn and back! How could we not be changed by that?"

"Yeah, I see your point. But he was inside our mind, messing around in our thoughts. You mean you're okay with that?"

She shrugged her shoulders as if that sort of thing happened every day. "The Professor wouldn't do anything to hurt us."

"That's pretty funny coming from you." Eric stopped chewing for a moment, trying to frame the words that he wanted to say to her.

"You saved my life tonight," he said, nervously playing with a corner of the blanket rather than looking at her.

"Technically, SID did the actual saving. And the Professor of course."

"Yeah, but SID couldn't have got to me in time if it hadn't been for you."

"You would have done the same for me," she said.

"How did you do it?" he asked. "Professor Strang told me that in order for the transfer to work, you had to have complete trust in the telescope and the person who created it."

"That's true."

"Then how did you do it?" he repeated. "I know you. That'd be like asking you to believe in fairies or something. You couldn't do that if you're life depended on it!"

"Hers didn't," said the Professor from behind them. Suddenly he was there, seated comfortably on the back of the couch.

"What did you say?" asked Eric.

"I said 'hers didn't'. But yours did. She would have done whatever it took to save you."

Eric hung his head. Meredith turned her face away to hide her embarrassment.

"When I invented the Discovery VII and the Chrysalis, I believed that I had made one of the most significant finds in the history of mankind. But in the last few hours the two of you have unearthed something far more important."

"We have?" Eric and Meredith spoke almost at the same time.

The Professor nodded. "You have learned that the most groundbreaking discovery, the most advanced technology, pales in comparison to the bond of comradeship and loyalty that the two of you have formed. Your friendship and trust in each other is the most powerful force in the universe."

Meredith and Eric looked at each other, their expressions solemn.

"And that's the secret isn't it?" asked Meredith. "Trust. You said it yourself."

She turned to Eric. "You could travel at the speed of thought because you trusted the Professor. And I," she gave their mentor an apologetic smile, "trusted you, Eric."

"You have unearthed something far more important."

"That's right," the Professor agreed.

"That means as long as we believe in you, and in SID, we can travel wherever and whenever we want. Right Professor?" asked Eric.

Their mentor's cheerless response took them by surprise. "I'm sorry, children. The Chrysalis has traveled for the last time." Hands in his pockets, head down, the Professor turned from them and stalked away.

"What?" Eric could not believe what he was hearing. "Can't you repair it? You said the Chrysalis was stored inside the computer. Can't you just, you know, make another copy of it?"

"Of course I can. But that's not what I meant. The Chrysalis has made its last journey," he repeated firmly.

"Professor, no!" Understanding what the Professor was really trying to say, Meredith spilled her plate in her haste to move to the Professor's side. "You can't mean that!"

"I can, and I do mean it! I cannot allow either of you to be exposed to the kind of peril that you faced tonight. 'You're always safe with the Professor?' I think not. The Discovery VII is far too dangerous. I'm never going to use it again."

"That's not fair, Professor!" Eric stood his ground. "I know SID said that the telescope has to be kept secret, but geez! It's the most awesome invention anybody ever thought of! And besides, I'm not afraid!"

"Then you're a fool!" The shocked look on the boy's face was more than enough cause for the Professor to regret his harsh words, but once uttered they could not be taken back. Nevertheless, his expression softened. "We must be logical about this, Eric," argued the Professor. "The scientific world was right. Children do not belong in space. What would I have told your parents if you had not come back from Saturn? How could I have explained to them that I risked your life on some wild goose chase?"

"Science is NOT a wild goose chase," shot back Meredith. "Science is man's search for truth; for meaning."

The Professor eyed the quick witted girl warily before replying. "Truth and meaning. An admirable pursuit for a scientist unless it results in a person's death, especially if that person is a child," he said pointedly.

"Then it was all for nothing," said Eric. "All the mystery, all the talk about dreams. For what? So you can stand there and tell us that you're giving up?"

"Yes, children. I must accept the responsibility."

"And what about your responsibility to David, to his memory?" asked Meredith. "Don't you owe it to him to go on? Isn't that what he would have wanted?"

Eric took a deep breath and tried to ask 'Who is David and what are you talking about?', but Meredith shot him a warning glance so he remained quiet and confused.

When Professor Strang finally spoke, his eyes were flashing.

"You don't understand!" he said, his voice ragged. "How could you possibly understand?'

It was Meredith's turn to stand her ground. Frightened, yet determined, she glowered up at him.

"I understand that you loved him," she said forcefully. Then her voice softened and her eyes brightened with tears of compassion. "And that you miss him terribly. But Professor, you can't just give up. David was an explorer. He would want you to finish what you started."

He stared at her in stony silence. Then he turned abruptly to the window, looking out but seeing nothing. Neither of the children dared to move or speak, reluctant to interfere with the Professor's thoughts. They knew that he was seriously considering everything they had said. He heaved a great sigh. As they waited, they saw his shoulders sag and he turned to face them.

"Finish what we started," he repeated quietly. "Yes, David would certainly approve of that. But the risk--!"

"Is ours to accept if we choose," said Eric. "Right or wrong, Professor, you got us into this. Whether you like it or not we're a team now, you and I, and Meredith and SID. We believe in you. It's time you started believing in us."

"Eric, you're starting to sound like SID." The Professor shook his head. "And I'm not sure I like it!" he added. He went to stand in the shadow of the great telescope, looking up at it thoughtfully. "Hmm. Changes would have to be made. Repairs, adjustments, some safety measures. A shorter jump, perhaps, a little closer to home," he muttered to himself. "Likely we'll trade today's mistakes for an entirely new set tomorrow. And there is the secrecy issue." He turned to them and said, "You children must understand that no one can know about SID, the telescope, or the Chrysalis."

"Like who'd believe us if we told them?" laughed Eric.

The Professor sighed again and ran his hands through his already rumpled hair. "All right, children. I will agree to think this matter over for a period of one week. I shall give you my answer then."

Unsure if their point had been won, the children exchanged hopeful glances.

"It's a deal." Eric stuck out his hand. The Professor looked at it thoughtfully before he extended his own, and solemnly shook the boy's hand.

"A deal, yes," he said. Then he offered his hand to Meredith as well, to seal the bargain all around.

"Young lady, have you ever considered someday becoming a lawyer?" he asked.

"Not on your life," Meredith replied with a grin. "I'm going to be an Astronomer!"

"Then heaven help us all!" laughed the Professor.

"I told you she could be hard to live with," Eric said.

She made a face at them both.

"Professor, the boy's mother is here," said SID.

"Well, my friend. Where have you been keeping yourself?" asked Professor Strang.

"I have been cleaning up the mess the three of you made," said SID patiently. "Believe me, it was considerable."

"What would I ever do without you, SID?" asked the Professor. "You're indispensable."

"Yes, I am," he agreed. "But don't think I didn't hear that remark you made earlier. Ordinarily I would be insulted at being compared to your new student, but in this case I hope he was able to talk some sense into you."

"You've been eavesdropping, SID," said Professor Strang. "That's very rude."

SID did not answer.

The Professor walked the children to the doorway. "Thank you for your help this evening, young lady. You were very brave."

"Thank you for bringing Eric back." Meredith reached up and hugged the Professor briefly but fiercely. Caught by surprise, he cleared his throat and backed hastily away as soon as she released him.

"You will remember your promise, won't you?" she asked.

The Professor smiled and nodded. Satisfied, she took the stairs two at a time, but Eric stopped to look back up at his mentor.

"Professor, are you all right?"

"Yes, Eric," he answered gently, "I'm fine. See you in a week."

Eric turned and disappeared after his friend.

* * * * * * *

It seemed strangely quiet in the observatory after the children had left. Professor Strang retrieved his digital companion from the computer workstation and climbed the ladder once again. Connecting SID to the telescope, his hands lingered on the cold metal tube. He adjusted the pedestal chair that he found handy for his long nightly sessions, and now he sat staring moodily at his own reflection shining up at him from the well polished brass.

"Professor?" asked SID.

"Yes," answered the Professor absently.

"Would you like me to dim the lights?"

"Yes, that would be fine. And open the dome, will you please?"

"Sure thing, Professor."

The Professor smiled as the massive ceiling of the observatory slowly and silently began to slide open. SID's agreeable comment had sounded a lot like Eric. He wondered if some of the boy's personality had rubbed off during the transference. SID would probably pitch another fit if I suggested that hypothesis, he thought. He decided against saying anything, for his little friend had been through enough that evening. They all had.

"What would you like to see tonight? I'll show you anything but Saturn."

"Don't worry, SID. I've had quite enough of Saturn for one evening. Shall we see if we can get lost in the Sombrero Galaxy?"

"Or maybe the Cat's Eye Nebula. We haven't been there for a long time."

"Why not look at both?" suggested the Professor.

"Good idea," said SID, and at his bidding the dome swung into the proper position. Except for the scratching of the Professor's pencil against his notepad, the observatory was silent for several minutes.

"Professor," SID hesitated. "Could I ask you something?"

"What's on your mind, my little friend?"

"Earlier, when you were talking with the children, you said something that I'm not sure I understand completely."

"Go on," the Professor encouraged.

"Well, you were telling them that their friendship was the most important thing in the universe. But I thought that, well, you've always told me that scientific discovery was of greater consequence than any other thing a man could devote himself to. You said that the Discovery was the greatest invention of all time, and that I -"

"What's on your mind, my little friend?"

"And so you are, SID. You are my ultimate creation. You are completely brilliant. But don't you understand? With all your intelligence and all your ability to gather and store information, still you are limited by your inhumanity."

The Professor adjusted the eyepiece to pull the nebula into clearer focus.

"You cannot understand the frailties of the human mind, the vulnerabilities that lead us to such great heights of joy, such depths of despair. It's these weaknesses that give us strength, our integrity as human beings! But you're getting there, SID. After all, you did actually make a mistake tonight. I believe that's a first for you."

"Ouch! Take it easy, Professor!"

"I'm sorry SID, but it's the truth, although it was not nearly as big as the mistake I made. Actually, you are quite fortunate not to be bothered with such things. As much as you'd like to be human, you can only simulate human feelings and reactions as I have programmed you to do."

"Are you kidding? I'm glad you created me this way. I've been inside those children's brains." SID's voice shuddered. "All mixed up with emotions! You can count me out!"

"Now, SID. I know it's difficult for you to accept this, but you can't operate the telescope without their help. You need those mixed up minds of theirs; without them the Discovery is only an ordinary telescope."

SID had no reply. The Professor was sorry he had spoken so bluntly.

"Don't take it so hard, SID. You're not forgetting, are you, that the telescope is equally commonplace without you? You are an essential component in the conversion of brain waves to energy, the transformation of matter to quantum particles. Remember, no SID, no jump. We were painfully reminded of that tonight!"

For the moment, the Professor's explanation seemed to satisfy the computer.

"One other thing worries me though, Professor. We frightened those two quite badly tonight. Do you think they will be back?"

"I know they will."

"How can you be so sure?" SID asked.

"Trust me." From the Professor's tone, SID knew that he had nothing further to say on that matter. He rotated the dome to a new location in the sky and the Professor returned to his silent viewing. After a while, he leaned back in his chair, yawned, and stretched his long limbs.

"Tired, Professor?" asked SID.

"Yes, although I hate to admit it. Having young people about the place again is very taxing."

"I rather enjoyed it," said the computer.

"I think you like teasing the boy, maybe? Or perhaps not having to do all the work yourself?"

"Yes!" said SID.

"Yes to which question?"

"Both!"

The Professor shook his head and laughed. "Well, regardless of the reason I enjoyed having them here, too. I believe that with Eric and Meredith around, there will seldom be a dull moment."

"Professor, I think you're right," SID said agreeably. The green lights on his display panel were lazily blinking off and on. Simulated or not, it was a sure sign that he was happy.

GLOSSARY

Note: Definitions found in this glossary are those which apply to the story. Many words have more than one definition.

****words created by the author to enhance the story***

abracadabra – word used by a magician to perform magic
adaptation – to adjust to changed conditions
adrenaline – a hormone produced by the body that causes the heart to beat faster
aeronautical – referring to the science of making or flying aircraft
aft – toward the back of a ship
Albert Einstein - A great scientist of the 20th century. He discovered the mathematical relationship between matter and energy.
altimeter – an instrument for measuring altitude or height above the earth
amidst – in the middle of
analyze – to study carefully in order to understand
Andromeda Galaxy – Earth's 'nearest' neighboring galaxy, approximately 2.26 light years away
animated – full of life and spirit
Apollo missions – NASA's manned missions to the moon from 1968 to 1975
apprentice – a beginner learning a craft or trade from an expert
Arthur C. Clarke - Sir Arthur Charles Clarke (born December 16, 1917) is a British author and inventor, probably most famous for his science fiction novel. For many years he was considered one of the Big Three of science fiction, along with Robert A. Heinlein and Isaac Asimov.

artificial intelligence – intelligence created by human beings
ascend – to go up
astronaut – a person who travels through outer space
astronomer – a scientist or other person who studies the stars and planets
astronomical – about astronomy, or very large
Astronomy – the study of stars, planets, or any object in outer space
atmospheric pressure – the weight of the air around us, 14.69 pounds per square inch at sea level
atmosphere – the air or gases surrounding a planet or moon
atmospheric composition – what the atmosphere is made up of
atmospheric density – the thickness or weight of the atmosphere
audible – can be heard
axis – the imaginary straight line that passes through the center of the Earth, around which it revolves.
ball bearings – small, loose, metal balls, heavy objects rest upon them so they can be moved
binoculars – an instrument used to see far off things, made for both eyes
Biology – the study of living organisms
Biotronic * – a combination of living and electronic material that depend on each other
blossomed – to bloom or flourish
bluff – a high steep bank
bookworm – someone who likes to read and spends much time doing it
Cassini Division - The Cassini Division is the main, dark division between Saturn's largest rings. This gap is 2,920 miles (4,700 km) wide and was discovered by Giovanni Cassini in 1675.
Cassini-Huygens mission - Cassini-Huygens (2004) is an unmanned space mission intended to study Saturn and its moons.

Cassiopeia – a constellation that looks like the letter W in the northern sky of North America near the Big Dipper, named for a Greek goddess who thought herself beautiful
Cat's Eye Nebula - The Cat's Eye Nebula (NGC 6543) is a planetary nebula in the constellation of Draco. Structurally, it is one of the most complex nebulae known, with high resolution Hubble Space Telescope observations revealing remarkable structures such as knots, jets and sinewy arc-like features.
caustic - sarcastic; cutting
celestial – something seen in the sky or in the heavens
chaos – the confusion of matter from which the universe is believed to have been created; utter confusion
charlatan – a fake
Chrysalis – in nature, a cocoon. * The name given to the space craft that one travels in during the translocation process
Class 4 * atmospheric probe – a device which measures atmospheric pressure and density
clean room – a laboratory or other area completely free of bacteria and dust particles
clock drive – a device that keeps a telescope centered on a target like a planet or galaxy
colossal – very large
compensate – to balance out, to make up for something else
component – a part of a larger object
computer console – the frame containing a computer and its controls
computer matrix – a combination of the hard drive and memory which allow a computer to operate
computerized – collected or stored electronically
conceited – vain or stuck up
conformed – to be like or in harmony with
constellation – a group or cluster of stars often named after a legendary or mythological character
convert – to change

Corvis – a constellation found in the southern skies of Northern America in springtime, named after a crow in Greek mythology
cosmic – referring to the universe as an orderly system
cosmonaut – Russian astronaut
Cosmosphere * - a space going craft that provides everything the traveler needs
CPR – Cardio Pulmonary Resuscitation – the process through which a person's respiratory and circulatory systems are kept functioning artificially until medical assistance is obtained
critical – fault finding
curvature – a bending or curving of a surface, in this case the surface of the Earth
dark adaptation – dark adaptation refers to how the eye recovers its sensitivity in the dark following exposure to bright lights
database – a gathering of information
Day the Earth Stood Still (the) – A 1951 movie in which an alien lands and tells the people of Earth that we must live peacefully or be destroyed as a danger to other planets. Great movie!
decontamination – to get rid of pollutants
degrees – a unit of measurement equal to 1/360th of a circle – the movement of the earth or of a telescope is measured in degrees
dematerialize – to reappear
demonstration – the act of showing someone how to do something or how something works
descend – go down
digital energy * – the potential or ability of numbers to create motion
dilation – when the irises of the eye become enlarged in a darkened environment in an attempt to gather more light
directional controls – the controls on the spacecraft that allow it to move forward and back, or from side to side
disembodied spirit – a ghost or other specter that has no physical body

disorienting – mentally confusing
dissect (dissection) – to cut up in order to study
divulge – to give up information
dynamic – referring to energy or motion; vigorous or productive
Edu-sci-fi ® * - educational science fiction
elements – components or essential parts
Emergency Medical Technician – a person trained to provide medical assistance in emergency situations
emotional stability – steadiness of feelings
emphatically – said or done with special force
environmental – referring in this case to the air, temperature, and gravity aboard a spaceship
escapade - reckless adventure
exhilarating – exciting or joyous
eyepiece – the viewing lens of a telescope
finder scope – a smaller telescope attached to a larger one, the observer uses it to help align the scope for viewing
formula – a set prescription of words or numbers; a recipe for doing or making something
galactic –referring to a galaxy
galaxy – a vast system of stars like the Milky Way Galaxy
gaseous nebula – a cloud of gas and dust in interstellar space or surrounding a star
Giovanni Cassini – a 17th century astronomer who explored Saturn through telescopes
gullible – easily fooled
hacked – cut up or chopped
haphazardly – casually or carelessly
heat proof shielding – material which, when applied to surfaces, protects from heat or fire
helium – a light inert gas
hydrogen – a flammable gas, colorless and odorless
hypothesis – a supposition or unproved theory
illusion – a false impression or misleading image
immune – exempt, not affected by
inconsistent – not in agreement

indispensable – something you cannot do without
inert – having no power of motion or action
inertia – an object at rest will remain at rest, an object in motion will remain in motion unless acted on by an outside force
informant – a person who discloses or reveals information
initiate – to begin to use
innovative – new or different
instantaneous – happening in a moment
integrated – having all parts brought together
interspersed – scattered between or among
interstellar – in between the stars
intricate – complicated or detailed
ion propulsion – a method of moving a craft through space using positively charged xenon atoms (xenon is a heavy gaseous element found in nature)
Isaac Asimov – a science fiction author, born 1920 (same year as my mom) whose writings include *I Robot*
jaunt – a short enjoyable trip
jeopardy – great danger
Jupiter –5th and largest planet in our solar system, named for a Greek god. Want to know more? Go to kidscosmos.org
kilometers – a unit of measurement; one kilometer equals about .6 of a mile
laboratory – a place where scientific experiments and research are carried out
legendary – founded on a myth or fable
lenient – merciful
Leonardo da Vinci – a 15th century inventor, artist, scientist; a Renaissance man
life support – all things which are needed for biological life to be maintained
light year – an astronomical unit of measurement; the distance which light travels in a year; 5,865,696,000,000 miles. WOW!

M13 – or Messier 13 – a cluster of stars found in the constellation Hercules. Charles Messier was a French astronomer famous for discovering and cataloging over one hundred deep sky objects.
M51 – also known as the Whirlpool Galaxy, really two galaxies in the process of colliding
magician – an expert in performing magical tricks or sleight of hand
magnetic fields – an area of force which surrounds a moving electrical charge
magnitude – the brightness of a star
malfunctioning – not working properly
manual control – controlled by a human being rather than a computer
mass – the amount of matter an object contains
matter to energy transfer * – this process is the result of a very imaginative mind and, unfortunately, not my original idea. Many science fiction writers have imagined that it might be possible to convert matter to energy, move it from place to place, and then change it back to matter again. If you ever figure out how to do it, please call me.
memory circuits * – the pathway along which memory travels within a biotronic brain
mentor – wise and faithful counselor or teacher
microscope – an optical instrument for magnifying very small objects
millimeters - a small unit of measurement; one millimeter equals approximately four hundredths of an inch
Mona Lisa – a famous painting by Leonardo da Vinci of a woman with a mysterious smile
moon – a natural satellite which revolves around a planet
Mr. Wizard – a scientific television show from the 1950's hosted by Don Herbert
mythology – the study of traditional stories about gods or heroes
nanites – microscopic machines
nano technology – the science of microscopic machines

NASA – the National Aeronautics and Space Administration
Neptune – eighth planet from the sun, forth largest in the solar system, named for Roman god of the sea
nerd – a dull person, interested in dull things, who leads a dull life – you get the idea!
neural pathways – the pathways of the nervous system
nuclear power - electric energy generated using heat produced by an atomic reaction
objectively – fair minded, not prejudiced
obligated – bound by a sense of duty or by a promise
observatory – a building equipped for astronomical research
optometrist – eye doctor
Orion – the hunter; a constellation containing the star Betelgeuse
Orion Nebula – a gaseous cloud in the 'knee' of the Orion constellation
panorama – a wide view in every direction
paralyzed – unable to move or act
particle density – the number of particles per square unit of matter
particle gel sampling matrix – a device which gathers particles from the atmosphere
pessimism – a habit of expecting the worst to happen
PhD – The degree of Doctor of Philosophy, a higher degree than an Honors or Masters degree, involving at least two and a half years of supervised research resulting in a thesis. PhD graduates may call themselves "Dr".
philosopher – a student of philosophy; a person with calm judgment and practical wisdom
photophobic – unable to bear direct sunlight
planetary – referring to a planet
planet – any body revolving around the sun
Pleiades – an open star cluster in the constellation Taurus, also known as M45 or the Seven Sisters
port – the left side of a ship

portfolio – a flat portable case for loose papers and drawings
potential – something that is possible but does not yet exist in reality
PowerPoint – presentation software that allows you to create slides, handouts, notes, and outlines
precision – the quality of being exact or accurate
predicament – a trying or difficult situation
property of inertia – see inertia
propulsion system – a system which provides a driving force
protrusions – things that stick out
proximity alert – an alarm which tells you if something is nearby
psyche – the mind as it governs the total human being
quadrant – a quarter section of an area, usually a circle
rational – reasonable
ratted out – tattled on
reek – an unpleasant smell
references – a person who can give testimony as to one's ability or character
regress – to move backward
rematerialize – reappear
Renaissance – a revival of art and learning in Europe which lasted from the 14th to the 16th century. A Renaissance man is someone learned in many subject areas; music art, the sciences.
repercussions – a result of effect of some event
retina – the inner coating of the back of the eye containing cells which are sensitive to light
Robert Heinlein – born in 1907, often called the Grand Master of science fiction writing
rocket fuel – a type of propulsion used to send rockets into space
rotate – to turn
Russian Cosmonaut – an astronaut of Russian nationality
sarcastic – biting or cutting humor

Saturn – 6th planet from the sun and second largest in our solar system
Saturn set – the point at which Saturn disappears below the horizon
scan – to examine carefully
Sci-fi – short for Science Fiction – fiction based on scientific fact
Series 2000 Interactive Database * – a made up name for SID, who is a computer containing much information that can talk to humans and other computers alike
SID* – Scientific Interactive Database; a smart alec computer invented by Professor Arthur J. Strang
Sir Charles Wheatstone – inventor of the stereoscopic viewer
snide – mean or underhanded
solar gel collector – a device which collects microscopic particles from space
Sombrero Galaxy – M104; a brilliant galaxy which resembles a high topped Mexican hat
sorcerer – a wizard or magician
spectral analysis - the analysis of geological phenomena (vegetation, soil deposits, etc.) by interpreting the variation in color values from imagery
spectrum - the complete range of colors in the rainbow, from short wavelengths (blue) to long wavelengths (red).
spiral galaxy - galaxy composed of a flattened, star-forming disk component which may have spiral arms and a large central galactic bulge.
star chart – a map of the stars which shows their location and magnitude
starboard – the right side of a ship
stargazing – looking at stars, galaxies or other night sky objects
station keeping - the practice of maintaining the position of a satellite or ship in orbit around a planet
stellar cartography - in astronomy, a term used to refer to the mapping of stars, nebula, and other interstellar phenomena.

stereoscopic viewer – A device which uses two photographs. One photograph represents the left eye, and the other the right eye. When the two photographs are viewed in a stereoscopic apparatus, they combine to create a single three dimensional image.
submariners – people who travel in submarines
sufficient – enough
super sleuth – a really expert detective
tachyon - A tachyon (from the Greek word meaning "swift") is a hypothetical (an idea based on an educated guess) particle that travels at faster than light speed.
talisman – an object that will ward off or guard against evil
tangible – real or having value
Taurus – a constellation best seen in January, name means bull, is one of the 13 signs of the Zodiac
telescope – A devise that uses lenses or mirrors to enlarge images of distant objects. Astronomers use telescopes to study planets and stars.
theologian –a person who studies God or other religious topics
thought transference * - the process of sending a human being through space by converting their brain waves into digital energy and attaching them to an outgoing tachyon beam. Only humans can do it and only SID can make it happen (with a little help from the Discovery VII and the Chrysalis!)
thruster – something which provides force to create motion
Titan – 13th and largest of Saturn's moons; has an atmosphere
transference – the act of moving something from one place to another
translation – to change something written or spoken from one language to another
travel at the speed of thought * - instantaneous travel through outer space; only possible through the use of the Discovery VII systems

traversing – moving across an object or a space
triangulate – to survey or locate by use of trigonometry
twilight – the faint light just after sunset
universe - everything that exists anywhere
unscrupulous – without principles; dishonest
Uranus – 7th planet from the sun and 3rd largest, discovered by William Herschel in 1781
veterinary – a person trained to provide medical attention to pets
vice – a fault, failing, or bad habit
vortex – whirlpool
Voyager I – first deep space unmanned probe to pass out of our solar system. Photographed Saturn in 1980
Voyager II – followed in Voyager I's footsteps. Photographed Uranus and Neptune.
warring – fighting
wheedling – to coax someone to do something
Yuri Gagarin – first man in space, orbited the earth for 90 minutes on April 12th, 1961
zeal - enthusiasm